SILENT THUNDER
A Civil War Story

ANDREA DAVIS PINKNEY

SCHOLASTIC INC.

New York Toronto London Auckland Sydney
Mexico City New Delhi Hong Kong

ACKNOWLEDGEMENTS

Special thanks to the following organizations and individuals for their research assistance:
Chelsea Equestrian Center; The College of Physicians Library, Philadelphia;
Julius Lester: Caroline Duroselle-Melish, reference librarian, historical collection,
the New York Academy of Medicine. And last, but certainly not least,
I owe tremendous gratitude to my editor, Donna Bray, and to art director Anne Diebel,
both of whom brought incredible brilliance and professionalism to the creation of this book.
Thanks, too, to Jerry Pinkney for a stunning cover.

ISBN 0-439-20688-X

12 11 10 9 8 7 6 5 4 3 2   1 2 3 4 5 6/0

Printed in the U.S.A.   40

First Scholastic printing, February, 2001

Map by Claudia Carlson

To Lynne and P.J.

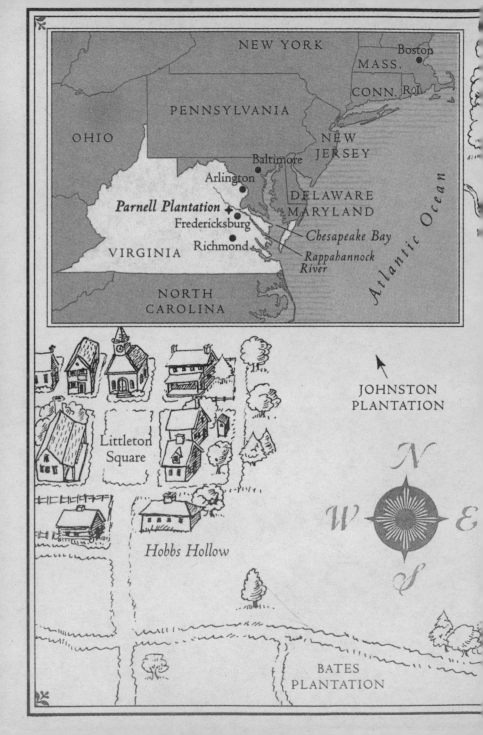

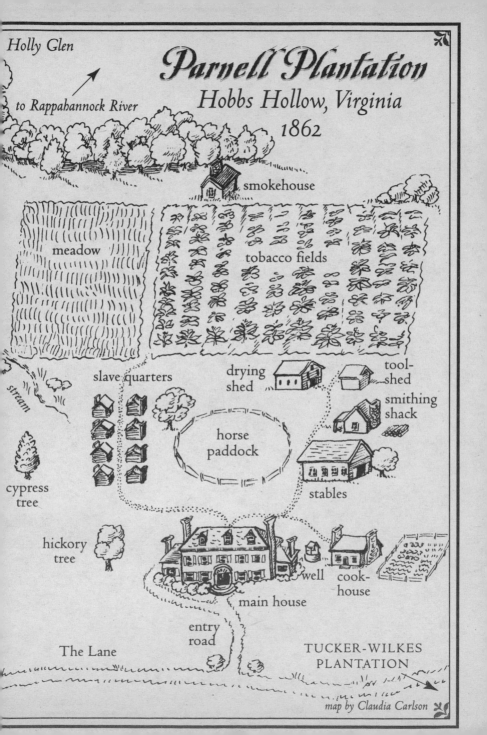

Holly Glen

to Rappahannock River

Parnell Plantation
Hobbs Hollow, Virginia
1862

smokehouse

meadow

tobacco fields

stream

slave quarters

drying shed

tool-shed

smithing shack

horse paddock

cypress tree

stables

hickory tree

well

cook-house

main house

entry road

The Lane

TUCKER-WILKES PLANTATION

map by Claudia Carlson

PART ONE

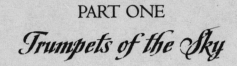

Trumpets of the Sky

1
Summer
August 21, 1862

EVERY YEAR WAS THE SAME. Come my birthday, he beckoned for me. He called for Rosco on his birthday, too. But Ros, anytime I raised it with him, he wouldn't speak on it.

Mama always made me wear my best—the calico dress she sewed for me to wear to Sunday services—and she scrubbed me till even my toe jam came clean. And Mama's orders to me never changed: "Don't go pestering him with all your foolish questions. And remember your manners."

Then she took me to the master's study, where she presented me to him. "Summer's come," she said simply. But even in her plain way of talkin', Mama put me in front of the master like she was making a proper introduction.

I'd been having these birthday look-sees in the

master's study for as long as I could remember. But every year—my birthday was the only day Master Gideon Parnell ever spoke to me—Mama presented me to the master as if he were meeting me for the very first time. Then she quickly left the study, carefully closing the large double doors behind her.

Master Gideon was seated at his desk. He looked as if he'd been waiting for me. "Come closer, Summer. Let me have a look at you." I made my way in slowly. He was nodding approval as I approached. I stopped just short of his desk chair. I suddenly remembered my manners, and gave a little curtsy. It was early morning, so the day's heat had not come on fully. It *would* come, though. Would come strong. Today the swelter seemed to be starting up in me, before it had poured over the air outside.

I'd been in Master Gideon's study plenty of times. Mostly, though, he wasn't in there when Mama and me were cleaning. There was something different about that study when the master was inside. He filled it somehow. Filled that place full of polished mahogany and heavy curtains. He made that dark, serious room get to be alive and breathing.

As I stood real still, waiting for Master Gideon to speak, he slowly lowered his eyes over the top of his reading spectacles. "You're getting to be a fine young lady, Summer. Girlhood's soon to be a memory to you," he said.

"Yessir." I smoothed my dress.

Seeing as the master didn't hardly pay me no attention any other time, I used these birthday visits to steal a close look at him. There was something in the master's face that tugged at me. Something that made me want to hang on when I looked at him. Seemed like I was always about to find something when I got to studying hard on his face. Could have been I felt that way 'cause the master's eyes didn't hardly leave mine whenever I went to him on my birthday. It was as if I were tugging at him, too. It was as if he were searching for a lost thing when he looked at me.

"Your mama ever tell you how you came by your name?" he asked.

"Born in the thick of summer, I was, here at Parnell's—at your plantation. Mama named me for them two things. Summer Parnell."

The master nodded.

"The name suits you, Summer. From what I can see, you've always been a bright child."

"Yessir. Thank you, sir."

I tried to say as little as I had to during these meetings. I worried that I'd disgrace Mama somehow, so the less I spoke, the better. The visits didn't last long before the master dismissed me. We usually exchanged brief courtesies, got to looking close at each other, then I'd leave.

But this year was different. This year, Master Gideon wasn't letting me go so fast. He was calling me bright, and talkin' about all kinds of things. And before I knew it, he was giving me a gift. He was giving me the gift of his words. The gift of more than the speaking of brief courtesies.

"Do you know why I come to this study, Summer?"

"It's your private quarters, sir. Your room for contemplation, Mama says."

The master smiled a little smile. "Contemplation." He nodded. His eyes left mine, but only for a moment. "This study's where I come to be among my books and papers, and my quill. It's where I find truths—in the pages of these many volumes."

Master Gideon turned to the bookshelves that flanked the large arched windows. That was the gift—his words. *Truths in the pages of these many volumes.* I'd been polishing the master's books ever since my fingers could hold a rag. Whenever I asked Mama what them books were for, and why the master had so many, she told me to mind my business and to keep with my work. Them books was something she refused to discuss.

But truth, now that was another story. Mama wasn't shy on talkin' about truth. Mama said when I was born I had a face like a hooty owl—wide-eyed, and always lookin'. A face searching for truth, even in darkness. I was hooty-eyed still, Mama said. Still searching, I guess. Got eyes the color of clover. Always thought maybe there was truth in everything green and new.

But it wasn't till that day in the master's study, my eleventh birthday, that the word *truth* stuck its burrs in me and held on tight. And it wasn't till that same day that my mind put truth and books into the same bailiwick.

The master had said he tried to fetch him some truth in all his pages and papers. But there was another kind of truth in that study, too. Something real and close and right. Something I didn't fully know. Something unspeakable.

Silence stood between Master Gideon and me. I had let my eyes drop, but I could feel the master's gaze resting right at my face.

"You're resembling your mama more and more, Summer."

"Yessir. I do favor her, sir."

"That's lucky, Summer, to look like Kit."

"Thank you, master."

My cheeks grew warm, and all of a sudden the collar on my dress started to itch. I'd told Mama the dress was getting too small, that I was growing past its seams, but she had insisted I wear it to see the master. Morning's heat was swelling fast all around now. The master took a kerchief from his breast pocket. He lifted his spectacles and wiped the bridge of his nose. "August in Virginia can be merciless," he said.

I went to the windows, tied back the curtains, and unlatched the window toggle to let in some air. When I returned to my place near the master's desk, Master

Gideon had turned open what to me looked like a ledger. And he'd taken up his quill. He turned to a clean page of the ledger and showed me its bare whiteness. "I call this book my index of memorable consequences. I write about those things that are most important to me. It's a record of daily memories, events, and circumstances I want to recount in my elder years."

The master dipped his quill. "That's all a fancy way of saying I keep a journal." He motioned with two fingers for me to come closer to the desk, close enough to see his journal better. All I could think of, again, were the master's words: *truths in the pages of these many volumes.*

Master Gideon wrote something at the top of the page. "I always start with the day's date," he said.

I watched carefully as the master's quill curled and scratched on the parchment. "You ever write about Mama?" I asked suddenly.

The master didn't answer, but I saw his hand flinch just the tiniest bit. He kept his eyes on his quill. He let my question pass like a fly on a breeze. He blew gently on the ink at the top of his page, then closed his journal.

It wasn't long before Master Gideon was sending me on my way, out into the merciless Virginia heat.

That night, as dusk fell on the quarters, Mama wrapped me in a hug. She thanked heaven for letting her see another one of my birthdays.

"I'm a lucky woman to still have both my children—none of them sold away, none of them beaten, both of them healthy as the shade trees that tower this land," she said.

But when I showed Mama the birthday present Rosco had given me, a hard look came to her. Mama and I had been butting heads ever since I could remember. The older I got, it seemed, the more we disagreed on things. There were times when we threw some heated words at each other, Mama and me. Tonight, when I saw the frown pinching Mama's face, I knew right away my book was going to put us at odds.

"Gideon give you that?" she wanted to know.

"Rosco," was all I said.

Mama shook her head. "Don't tell nobody 'bout that thing, Summer. Don't even speak to the leaves about it, you hear me?" she warned.

"How come I can't?"

"'Cause if the wrong people find out you got a book, you'll be sold off, or worse."

"*What* wrong people? Master Gideon ain't never gonna know. He don't hardly take notice on me—except on my birthday. Other times he don't even know I'm alive."

"He knows," Mama said firmly.

"If it ain't my birthday, he don't so much as look my way."

"He's busy running this plantation, is all."

I fingered the pages of my book. "Does the master call *you* to him on *your* birthday?" I'd never thought to ask Mama that before, but now it seemed such a sensible question.

"No," Mama said.

"How come?"

"He don't know when my birthday is," she said softly.

"Why don't you tell him—then he'll know."

Mama folded her arms tight. "Hush up," she said.

"You're *always* trying to hush me."

"That's 'cause you're a bottomless well of questions, child. You run too deep with too many how-comes and why-nots. It's a pestering menace."

I was holding my book close to me now. As close as breathing, it seemed.

"I just don't want you to make a silly mistake and go bragging to folks about that thing. You know how talkedy you can get."

I didn't tell Mama that Rosco had promised to learn me letters, had promised to learn me to read with the book he'd stolen from young Master Lowell.

Rosco was the only one of us who had been learned to read. "That boy knows way too much for a thirteen-year-old child," Mama says.

Rosco taught himself to know words. He did it by listening to Lowell, Master Gideon's boy, practicing his lessons. You see, Rosco was Lowell's own body servant; Rosco *belonged* to Lowell. He polished Lowell's shoes, shined his door brass, put Lowell's bedwarmer between his sheets when the colder months came on, mucked the stall where Dash, Lowell's gelding, stayed, and did any other chores Missy Claire, the master's wife, wanted him to do for Lowell.

It wasn't regular for a boy to have a slave child of his own. Heck, Lowell couldn't have been no more older than Rosco—twelve, maybe thirteen years old. But I heard Mama tell her friend Thea that Master Gideon gave Rosco to Lowell because Lowell was sickly. He had some kind of breathing trouble, which was why he was always wheezing like a pup, hungry for air. Lowell's wheezy breathing could have been why he was so skinny—and so *pale*.

Anyway, ever since Miss Rose McCracken, the white teacher lady, had been coming to Master Gideon's study to learn Lowell to read, Rosco had been stealing looks at Lowell's lesson books. Rosco said whenever he could hear Lowell reading out loud, he listened real close. Then later, when Lowell was out in the courtyard taking his afternoon refreshment, Rosco looked at Lowell's lesson books and, one by one, had learned the letters for himself. Rosco said he first started doing this two summers ago.

When I asked Rosco how he learned so good, he said it took him many days of quick, eye-dartin' glances before he began to catch on, and more time on top of that before he could fully read. He said the dim light of

Lowell's room forced him to look real hard at them letters till they started to make sense—till they grew into full-out words.

Well, once, after Lowell was done with one of his lesson books—Rosco said it was a book called *The Clarkston Reader*—Lowell set it on the shelf in Master Gideon's study. One day Rosco swiped the book right off the shelf, slid it under his shirt, brought it back to the quarters, and taught himself to read it full and well—from the very front to the last page!

Then Rosco got the boldness of a bloodhound in him, swiped himself a page from Lowell's writing tablet, and learned himself to make letters.

When Mama found out Rosco had stolen from the master's son, she begged him to put the stuff back. Her eyes had tears in them—that's how serious she was about it. But Rosco, he said no. He went against Mama, just like that.

By the time night fell, the dander had settled between Mama and me. Mama said, "I know we have our share of clashes, Summer. And I have true concern about that book. But I'm not one to deprive a child of her birthday present. You can have the book so long as you promise to keep it hid away."

"I promise, Mama," I said.

Later, after everyone had gone to sleep, Rosco came close to my pallet and whispered to me, "Now it's your turn, Summer. It's your turn to learn letters, and I'm gonna teach you. That's your real birthday present from me—from your brother Ros, the smartest slave boy on Parnell's place."

Then Rosco tucked Lowell's hard, thin book under my head. "Dream big, now," he said. "We'll start our lessons soon. Happy birthday, Summer."

I fell asleep happy and itchin' to get started with my lessons. But I kept hearing Mama's warning about my learning book.

"*. . . keep it hid away.*"

2
ROSCO
August 24, 1862

THE BIT.

It's choking me.

Choking back my breath.

Only breathing I can do is through my nose. But that breathing hurts. It hurts to smell the leather and iron, soaked with the foam from my spit.

Then comes the worst of it. He's yanking on the bit. Stretching my lips and jaws into an ugly, messed-up grin. Snatching back my neck. Sending my eyes rolling. Rolling bald and blinded, way far back in my head.

I can't fight the bit. Ain't never been able to break free from its iron hold.

I get still and quiet. Throat burning. Limbs gone to mush.

He's ready to mount me, now that I'm still. Mounts me bareback. Doesn't even bother with the saddle.

My insides are screaming, "Buck! Buck 'im off!" But I'm goose-flesh all over. Helpless.

Soon his face is down near mine. His mouth right at my ear. The breath on him is hot and stinky—like a sick, mad dog, just come from slopping swamp water. Now he's hollering crazy-like, "Come on, nigra boy, take me for a ride!" His boot heels dig hard into my gut. "Giddy-up!" he shouts. And then he's riding me full-out.

I try, best I can, to twist my head back around. Try to see his face. But there ain't no way to twist. He's got me reined up tight.

I know his voice, though. It's the ugly voice of slavery. It's the cruel call of every white man who enjoys his ride on the back of a nigra.

I'm able to see my feet making a slow gallop. My feet are bare. Thick with mud. The longer I look, the more I see they ain't feet at all. My toes have grown together. They've grown hard.

Just as I see them swelling, turning to hooves, I hear Mama calling me, soft and low.

"Rosco! Rosco, child, wake up! You're dreaming haints again." Mama was holding me to her. Soon as I felt her hands cupping both my cheeks, I knew the ride was over—over for now, at least. These evil dreams haunted my sleep on too many nights. And each time, Mama was there to deliver me from them. "I'm here," she said. "Easy, now."

"It was night terrors again, Mama," I explained, sitting up, trying to shake myself free of the dream.

"Them dreams is just demons," Mama said. "Don't let 'em get the best of you, child."

I shifted on my pallet. As much as I liked the

feel-good warmth of Mama's hug, I tried to gently twist free of her hold. Sissies let their mamas hug them in the night. I was thirteen, almost a man. Too old for letting demon dreams scare me.

Still, I listened close to Mama as she told me what to do when haints came to my sleep. "Darkness has a way of making demons seem real," she said. "When them haints come creepin', petition the Almighty with one word—any word at all—to soothe your soul in that very moment. Say it over and over, till peace comes."

I sure as heck didn't know how a word could turn back demons, but I nodded when Mama spoke. I nodded like I understood. To my way of thinking, it was Mama herself—Mama's strong arms holding me, that sure way Mama had of talkin'—that drove them demons away from my dreams.

"Best way to feel safe in darkness is to speak words that comfort you," Mama said.

That morning I went to town to help my friend Clem, Master Gideon's tack slave, load horse-shoeing iron onto the flatbed of the master's wagon. It was then that I spotted me a page from something called *Harper's Weekly*, rustling past my ankles on the dirt. My eyes caught the words *free* and *slave*.

You never saw me snatch a scrap of trash off the ground so fast. (I'm good at quick swipes—been swiping Lowell's tablet paper and books out from Master Gideon's study ever since I was little). Clem was too busy sizing up his shoeing iron to notice me crumpling the *Harper's Weekly* into the seat of my drawers, but I could feel that sharp-cornered ball of paper pressing into the skin on my backside all the way home. Felt like a burr pricking at me, only bigger.

Later, I stole off to the cypress tree that marks the edge of Parnell's land, so's I could get quiet and be alone. I read every one of that paper's words. I even read words I ain't never seen the likes of before that day. Words like *rebellion* and *authorized*. There was one sentence, though, that I read without a hitch. It said that henceforth, all slaves admitted into military service are declared free, along with their wives and children.

It also said that colored men could fight to help turn back slavery, and that President Abraham Lincoln was under something called *coercion* to free *all* black people to destroy the Confederacy, and win the war.

Boy, did that paper get my head to spinning. Me, a solider—fighting to be free. It was a high-headed notion that had crossed my mind a time or two. But seeing it spelled out, all clear and official, put a whirl of excitement in my belly.

To go off to fight would have meant that I'd have to leave Mama and Summer. But it also meant I could get out from under Master Gideon's rule, and that I wouldn't have to take care of young Master Lowell anymore.

I had promised Summer I'd teach her to read, and goodness knows, she'd have had a hissy fit if I just up and went off and didn't keep my word. And Mama, she thought any kind of fighting was not the Christian way, even though I'd tried telling her that this war was what could make all of us free. When I said that, Mama just shook her head. I swear, sometimes I thought my very own mother liked busting her backbone for white people.

Mama didn't know about me wanting to fight. Neither did Summer. Thea knew, though. She knew everything, without even having to ask. She had what Mama called "the power of intuition." But to me it was more than that. Thea could see inside people's thoughts. That's why we called her a *seer*. Sometimes she told me what I was thinking before I knew I was thinking it myself. Like on that very afternoon, after I had tucked the scrap from *Harper's Weekly* back in my britches and was coming up to Master Lowell's quarters, thinking on enlisting. Thea met me on the road. She took a solid look at me. "You got the war drum beatin' in you, don't you, child?" was what she said. All's I could do was nod.

I sure wished Thea could put thoughts *in* people's heads instead of just take them out. That way, she could have stricken Mama with a clear notion that slavery was as far off from any kind of Christian way that there was, that freedom was what the Almighty had in his mind when he created this world.

3
Summer
August 27, 1862

THE BOOK ROSCO GAVE ME sure smelled funny. Smelled like a horse saddle and sawdust, all rolled into one. That thick odor filled my nose all night long while I tried to sleep. I tossed on my pallet, thinking about learning letters from Rosco, thinking about how someday I'd be able to make sense of all them black squiggles Mama said don't look like nothing but chicken scratch.

I woke at twilight, before I heard Chief, the cock, crowing. The sun hadn't even opened its eyes yet, but, oh, I was wide awake.

But this morning, as soon as I saw even the smallest crack of light entering the sky, I slid Rosco's book—well, Lowell's book that Rosco swiped—out from under my head and turned it open. Them black squiggles were truly beautiful, all lined up one after the other, marching like tiny, fancy dancers across the pages. I slowly ran my finger over that parade of squiggles. "*Letters*," I whispered.

Inside the book's hard front cover there was a swirl of letters, too. Them letters were even fancier still. They were curly, and looked as though they'd been drawn with a quill like the one I saw the master use in his study. Looked like swells of water that slosh and dip in Mama's washbasin, like I could dive right into them and let their eddies take me for a ride.

Soon as I heard Chief's call, I slid my birthday present back under my pallet and closed my eyes, like I was fast sleeping, like I'd never woke. Not long after, Mama came and shook me. "Summer—Summer, child, wake up!"

I didn't like lying to Mama, but today I didn't feel like waking. I wanted to enjoy the dreamy thoughts I was having about the letters in my book. So I faked sleep real good. To my way of thinking, I wasn't really lying (lying's done with words); I was just fooling Mama.

"Why does morning always come on so quick?" I asked, burying my face.

"'Cause that's the way God made things," Mama said simply.

I kept my face hidden, and couldn't help but smile to myself. Mama really thought I was 'sleep!

Later, it was hard for me to keep my book hid all day while I was pounding bread dough 'longside Mama in the cookhouse. I kept wanting to go back to the quarters, kept wishing I could pull my book out from under my pallet and look at it—at those curly dancers.

But by late afternoon my mind was far gone from thinking 'bout my book. Missy Claire came fluttering into the cookhouse like she'd been bit by a bumblebee. "Kit, Kit, bring a steam pot," she squawked. "Bring it quick!"

Kit's my mama, and whenever Missy Claire spoke Mama's name, she dragged it out real slow, made it sound like a long word rather than a short one. *Keee-at*—that's how she said it.

When Missy Claire called Mama, a frown took over Mama's face, same look as when I showed her the book Rosco gave me. A knowing, worried look.

See, whenever Missy Claire hollered for Mama to fetch a steam pot, it was 'cause young Master Lowell's lungs had gone tight, and he was struggling to breathe. Mama boiled the water in a stew pot and took it to Lowell's room.

Even though Rosco was Lowell's body servant, it was Mama who knew best how to stop Lowell's wheezing spells. Today, like always, she poured the steaming water into the basin next to Lowell's bed, draped Lowell's head in a muslin hood, and spoke real soft to Lowell, like she was coaxing a frightened lamb.

Missy Claire always stood back and let Mama do the soothing. Mama spoke gently. "Pull your breath in through your nose, child, then let it out slow from your mouth."

Missy Claire stayed behind Mama, looking scared. Lowell was coughing and gasping and whimpering, seemed like all at the same time. Finally, he was breathing regular again. Mama led his head back from the steam and rested it on the pillows she had propped behind him.

Lowell's face glistened from the steam water and from his own sweat. Mama's face was shiny, too. They'd both been working hard.

Missy Claire dabbed Lowell's face with the muslin. "I'll tend to him, now, Kit," she said to Mama. But it was Mama who had freed Lowell's lungs, not Missy Claire. Missy's tendin' to her son was mostly just sitting by his side, shaking her head, pressing her palm to her cheek.

"Ever since that child been a baby, I been tellin' Missy Claire to treat him with cayenne liniment. It won't cure Lowell, but it would cut down on them attacks," Mama said when we were back in the cookhouse and she was dumping Lowell's steam water out the back door. "Missy Claire has always been a woman who's set on having the final say." Mama sighed. "She insists that well water, boiled up hot, is enough for Lowell."

I sure had better things to think about than Missy Claire's stubborn ways. I turned my thoughts back to my book, back to them pretty, swirly quill curls.

4
ROSCO
September 1, 1862

THEY SAID IT WAS a white man's war. But if that was
true, how come Master Gideon waxed on about "the
condition of slavery" and "preserving the slave way"
whenever he got to talking about this war they called
"the War between the States?" Seemed to me that anything having to do with slavery would surely include
nigras. I had never in my life seen a white man who was
a slave. So to say this war was only the white man's
struggle was a bunch of swine-slop.

Now, don't get me wrong 'bout Gideon Parnell. He
was better than most masters. He had a reputation for
being one of the most even-tempered masters this side
of Richmond. Sometimes, though, he could be downright opinionated. That's 'cause Master Gideon Parnell
was a true Secesh if I ever did see one. Secesh through
and through—lived and breathed for the South.

If ever the North seemed to have one up on what he called "our beloved Southern soil," the master's eyes turned greener than a field of envy.

At least Gideon's eyes weren't filled with the hatred I'd seen peering out from other white men. But the sad thing was this: When it came to Lowell, the master could be as coldhearted as they come. I had never seen a man talk about his own son the way Gideon Parnell talked about Lowell.

You'd have thought Lowell was the nigra of one of them cotton-country masters, the way Master Gideon put him down, knocked at his pride, and cursed him at every turn. Made me feel nothin' but pity for Lowell. Made me want to tend to him with as much kindness as I could manage.

That boy had everything I didn't—hard-soled shoes, a feather bed, and a teacher lady to show him books. But he didn't even have what it took to fight for his own breath. That was a soul-sorry shame, if you asked me.

But for all the talking Parnell did *about* his son, he didn't ever talk *to* him. Really, I had never heard him say a single word to Lowell—not a one! It was as if Lowell was dead. Or like he just wasn't here in this world.

Truth is, Master Gideon probably talked to *me* more than he even talked to his own boy. That was a sad state of things, since the master didn't hardly pay me no mind, except for once a year on my birthday, when he had Mama bring me to his study for a look-see.

Like with Lowell, the master was blind to me every other day of the year. I sure hated them birthday look-sees, hated feeling like I was an auction horse on display. Far as I knew, Summer and me were the only ones Master Gideon called on this way. Somethin' strange about it. That's why I never spoke 'bout them birthday visits to nobody. Even though the master was civil when we met, looking on him so close—and having him take to looking at me—always put a shudder on my insides.

But at least on one day out of a whole bunch of planting and harvesting seasons, the master would grant me a word or two. Heck, as uneasy as I felt about them birthday meetings, I knew that even a horse needs talkin' to from his master, every now and again.

You'd have thought Lowell would try to get his pa to speak to him by speaking to his pa. Maybe asking his pa some kind of important question so he'd *have* to answer. But Lowell was as tight-tongued toward Master Gideon as Master Gideon could be toward him. He didn't hardly say nothin'. Even when he was telling me to do something, it came out all soft and whispery, with no more than a few words at a time.

And to make it worse, Lowell's words got all tangled up on his tongue before they came out. *Stuttering* is what I'd once heard Miss McCracken, Lowell's teacher, call it. But when Miss McCracken asked Lowell to read out loud during his lessons, he had the most clear way of speaking that I ever did hear from a boy my own age. It was as if his books made him strong, somehow.

Today I was mucking the hay in Dash's stall when I heard Master Gideon telling Horace Bates, the county doctor who'd come to check on the master's gelding, Marlon, that Lowell was nothing but "a lump of coal that's smeared the Parnell name." (Doc Bates was an all-purpose medicine man. He tended people, mostly, but knew a good lick about animals, too.)

Master Gideon knew I was mucking right near where he was, but that didn't stop him from speaking his true mind about his son. That's something I never fully understood about white people—the master, Missy Claire, and the few others I knew. They talked about private things straight-out, like nigras were some kind of mutes who couldn't hear a word they said.

I was looking down at my pitchfork and clearing the hay of Dash's droppings while I listened to Parnell.

"My boy's a runt. Nothing but a measly bag of bones and poor lungs. Claire and me, we've been cursed, I tell you. Cursed with a sick-bodied child." Master Gideon sucked on his teeth as he spoke. The way somebody sounded when they were fed up. He seemed to be caught in his own thoughts, just talking out of his head.

"Every man in the Confederacy who's got a boy old enough to fight has sent that boy off to uphold the South's rightness. And you can best believe that anybody who's got a boy out there fighting is bragging to high heaven about it. Just yesterday I was coming out of the town council meeting, passing by Littleton Square, when I ran into Travis Stokes and Nathan Wilcox. All they could talk about was their sons 'putting their lives on the line for the flowering South.'"

Master Gideon let loose a sigh. "And then," he said, "Stokes had to rub salt on my sore by pulling out a letter his boy, Ben, sent home from the Battle of Shiloh. Stokes, that braggart, was waving that confounded letter around like it was the Confederate flag!"

Marlon, the master's horse, blew out soft breaths against his horse lips while Doc Bates examined him. "Not every boy is meant to be a solider," Doc Bates said.

Master Gideon sniffed. "Horace, we got Union soldiers closing in every day. And every man in this county who's got a son of war age is talking proud about his boy out there protecting our Southland."

Then the master did something I ain't never heard him do. He spat. "Besides," he said, "you know I've had my eye on a seat in Congress for as long as I can remember. It's hard enough being the only member of the town council whose boy is not putting in for the war. If someday I'm to represent the state of Virginia's better interests, I must free myself of anything that's considered objectionable—of anything that would prevent me from winning the confidence of the majority."

Doc Bates didn't say nothing right away. I could hear

Marlon's hooves crunching the hay beneath them. The doc spoke like he was losing his patience with Parnell. "Your son is not objectionable, Gideon. He's got an affliction that has little to do with your ability to win people's confidence," he said. Marlon let out a quick, tiny neigh. "This horse has got colic," Doc Bates said plainly.

It was as if Master Gideon hadn't heard Doc Bates's words. He was still deep in his own agitation. He said, "The Union's got nigras fighting for them, you know—escaped slaves. And now I'm hearing that just this month the War Department authorized General Rufus Saxton, some military governor of the South Carolina Sea Islands, to organize five regiments of black troops on the islands." Parnell got a desperate sound in his voice. "This letting nigras fight so close to home makes me uneasy," he said. "I guess I should take comfort in the fact that they're still slaves, living under Southern law. What a shame it would be to let them South Carolina coloreds think they got a chance at freedom. I hear them nigras up North think being soldiers is going to set them free."

Now I was listening close. You never saw me muck a stall so slow, so's I could hang around and hear all of what Master Gideon was saying. If I'd have been a horse, my ears would have flung forward right then. I even raked Dash's hay just a bit more quietly. I didn't want to miss a word.

Doc Bates spoke next. "Well, Gideon, I'll say one

thing about coloreds. They sure got a way of sticking together. If all the coloreds in Virginia put their minds to it, they *could* have an army of their own . . ." Doc Bates's words trailed off into a moment of silence. Then he said, "It ain't such a far-off notion."

Master Gideon sounded a single huff, like he was quickly dismissing Doc Bates's theory.

"Don't worry, Gideon, I was just speculating," Doc Bates said. "And don't get yourself all worked up over some crazy Union antics."

Both men were silent for what seemed like a long moment. I rustled more hay to give off the sound of hard work.

"General Grant *may* be full of wild ideas for his Union troops," Parnell said, "but his boys captured Vicksburg not more than a few weeks ago. Some thirty thousand of our soldiers surrendered there—thirty thousand!"

I could hear the disgust in Parnell's voice. He went on in a flurry. "I hear folks are saying that the Union's victories at Port Hudson and Milliken's Bend—where a whole bunch of nigras fought—helped seal Grant's success at Vicksburg. And now them Yanks got control of the Mississippi Valley."

That's when I heard Master Gideon clear his throat. It was as if he were about to make some big announcement. But when he spoke again, he spoke real low, real soft, not like he was hiding his words, but like he was ashamed of what he was about to say. "But I'll say this—and I'll only say this to you, Horace, seeing as we've known each other since the cradle—even if them nigra soldiers are falling all over themselves, at least they're *in* the war, and that's more than I can say for my own flesh and blood. Imagine it, coloreds to arms!"

I could hear Doc Bates closing up his medicine bag. "Don't put yourself into a dander about it, Gideon. Vicksburg was a noteworthy victory for Grant's army, I'm not denying that. But worrying doesn't solve anything."

Doc Bates and Master Gideon passed Dash's stall, where I was making like my hay-pitching was serious business. The two men didn't so much as glance in my direction. Doc Bates had a hand on Parnell's hefty shoulder. "Marlon will be just fine so long as you keep him active. If the colic persists, feed him a little mineral oil."

I peered through the barn slats, watching the doctor and Master Gideon make their way back toward the entrance road to Parnell's place. "I wish you had a potion in that bag that could cure my boy," Master Gideon said.

"A healthy dose of kindness can work wonders for a sickly child. Talk to your boy, Gideon. It sure can't hurt him."

Parnell shrugged. Doc Bates mounted his horse. Master Gideon gave the horse a gentle hind-slap, and watched the doctor ride away.

All's I could think on then was what I'd seen in *Harper's Weekly*, about black men being allowed to enlist in the Union army, and gaining their freedom once they did. Even though Gideon had gone on and on about Southern black troops who were not free, the master's protest was the promise of possibilities.

"Imagine it, coloreds to arms!"

5
Summer
September 10, 1862

ROSCO AND I FINALLY GOT to starting on our
lessons. We met behind the quarters, right before dusk,
near the cypress tree. I slid my book from the croaker
sack where I'd been keeping it hid. "This here's the best
present ever, Rosco," I said. "You know what the
master told me 'bout books when I went to see him on
my birthday?"

I was all ready to tell Rosco everything about this
year's visit with the master, when he held out a hand to
shush me.

"We *ain't* here to talk about *that*," he said. Rosco
lifted the book from my hands. He pushed it back
down in its sack. "Put this away," he said. "We need to
start with explaining, before we get to full-out book
learn'ng."

"But, Ros—" A swell of disappointment started to

rise in my belly. I'd been touching on my book's pages—and feeling the hardness of its cover under my head at night—long enough!

"Hold your horses, Summer." Rosco put a little squeeze on my arm. "Like Mama's always tellin' us, we got to take first things first." Then Rosco said, "Show me your leg, high up."

"*Ros!*" I was gettin' all up-jumpy. "You playing a trick on me? 'Cause if you are, it ain't no bit funny!"

Rosco's face was serious. "This is no silly foolin', Summer. It's our first lesson in letters. Now, slide your skirt up so's I can see where your leg meets your hip-bone."

I knew Rosco would never wrong me. He was as honest as the sun (well, he was mostly honest, 'cept for when it came to swiping books and tablet paper). And sometimes he had a strange way of explaining things. "All right, Ros." I agreed. "I'll lift my skirt, but I'm stopping soon as I get to my unders," I said firmly, sliding my skirt.

"Okay, that's good." Rosco held up his palms. "Now, what you see there?"

I was truly confused. "All's I see is my leg, sitting out like a prime target for a hungry mosquito looking for some flesh to chew on," I huffed. "This is a silly way to learn to read, Ros!"

"Keep looking," was all Rosco said.

I stared down at my knee and started to fidget. Then

Rosco pointed to the old scar up near my hip. He said, "Learning to read starts with letters. You got your own letter right on you. It's the sixteenth letter of twenty-six. The letter *P*."

I touched the spot on my thigh where the skin was puckered and raised and dark. "I been having that old scar on me since forever, Ros. That don't look a thing like what I seen on young Master Lowell's learning book. Why are you bluffing me so, Ros?" I clicked my tongue.

"You got that scar from the master himself. I got me one, too." Rosco yanked down the top of his britches to show me a hip scar that looked just like mine: *P*.

Then he yanked up his drawers and folded his arms tight in front of him. "*P* is the first letter of the master's family name—*Parnell*. It's a brand that tells people Parnell owns us. I've had my brand forever, too, Summer. We both got ours when we was babies, too little to remember the sore."

My skirt was still up to my hip. I studied the scar— the *brand*, the *P*—on my leg. "Sore?" I asked.

"The burn sore," Rosco said. "White people take a red-hot iron and burn the brands right into us, like we's their animals."

"Mama got a brand—a *P*—too?" I asked.

Rosco nodded. "Every slave on this place got a *P*— Mama, Clem, Thea."

My mind was back to racing with all those pretty letters from Lowell's lesson book. I wanted to be looking at *them*, not at some old natty scar on my leg. Even if the scar—the brand—*was* a letter, I sure didn't see the same beauty in it as I saw when I looked at them curlies in my book. I slid my skirt down over my leg, back to where it belonged. Rosco must have sensed my jumpiness. He took up my book from where it had been resting in the dirt and opened it to the front. I could feel my impatience start to ease. As soon as Rosco turned open my book, I let my eyes dance along the curves of them fancy letters on the book's inside cover, the ones made with quill ink. "Beautiful," I whispered. "What's it say, Ros?"

"Says Lowell Farnsworth Parnell. That's young Master Lowell's full name."

"All them swirls for *Lowell*?"

"Somebody—maybe Lowell himself—wrote it all out in the finest ink," Rosco explained.

"It swirls like the pattern on Missy Claire's china." I was staring hard at Lowell's name, taking it in. "Young master sure is lucky to have his name lookin' so fine," I said softly.

Rosco turned to my book's first page. There stood that pretty row of letters, staring back at us.

"You see this?" Rosco ran his finger along the bottom of the row.

"It looks like a parade. A happy parade, all lined up for a march," I said.

"This here's the *alphabet*. It's all the letters that make words."

Now I was touching the book, but not with just my finger. I was rubbing on it with the whole palm of my hand. "What does all this parade of letters *say?*"

"The alphabet's not a word, Summer. But you can take it apart—take two or three or four or ten letters from the alphabet, put 'em together in all kinds of different ways, and make a whole mess of words."

I turned through the pages of my lesson book, showing Rosco how the letters, and words, and *alphabet* danced when I fanned the pages real fast. "Let's put some letters together—*now*, Ros." A bunch of lesson time had gone by already, and I still didn't know one iota 'bout how to read!

Rosco said, "Words'll come, Summer." Then he turned back to the place in my book that held the parade of letters, the alphabet. "You see anything here that looks like your brand scar?" he asked.

I studied the letters from front to back, and back again. Some letters were tall and lean, others round and fat. One was sharp and pointed, like the tip of the paring knife Mama used to peel apples for a pie. I didn't see nothing that looked like my leg scar—like mine and Rosco's scar.

"It ain't here," I said.

"Keep looking," Rosco encouraged. "If you ever gonna learn to read, you first got to learn to stick with it when it starts gettin' hard."

I nodded. "*All right*, Ros, but I just don't see nothin' that looks anything like—" and before my impatience got the best of me, I saw the letter—the *P*—standing right up in the middle of the alphabet parade. "There it is, Ros!"

"What I tell you?" Rosco said.

That *P* was just as proud. It was nestled between two circles; one of the circles had a line poking out from it. "That's how my leg must've looked sticking out to the right, from my dress, ready for a mosquito to bite it," I said, pointing to that round, one-legged letter.

"That's *Q*, comes after *P*, in the alphabet," Rosco explained.

"*Q*," I repeated, tracing the letter with my finger. "What words can you make with a *Q* and a *P*?" I wanted to know.

"Ain't no words you can make with just a *P* and just a *Q*. You need other letters woven between the two of them before they can be turned into a word."

Fireflies had begun to spark the darkness. "We best get back to the quarters, Summer. Thea's gonna be starting evening prayers soon."

"But I don't know nothin' 'bout reading yet, Ros," I protested, turning through the pages of my book a second time. "All's I know is what a *P* and a *Q* look like, and them two letters together don't even make no words."

Rosco clapped his hand onto my shoulder, same way I seen him do to Dash when Dash gets riled up. "Girl, you jumpin' past the gate too fast," Rosco said. "Remember, it took me a long time of studying that book before I could even know a few little bitty words."

"But—" I began.

"But nothin'," Rosco interrupted. "Tonight at prayers you need to ask whoever it is Thea prays to to put some kind of patience in you." Rosco stood and held out a hand to help me up off the grass. "And pray to calm that flutter-bug that's batting at you." Rosco started to walk toward the quarters. I followed after him quickly.

"There ain't no flutter-bug batting at me, either! I got me plenty of patience," I snapped.

As we made our way back to the quarters, Rosco promised me that we'd stick with our lessons, that we'd meet under the cypress tree every time we could both steal away without anybody knowing we were gone. I could see the glow of Mama's prayer candle coming through the burlap that hung at the door of our cabin. The burlap was there to let in any little bit of night breeze that might float by, and to keep the bugs outside, away from where we slept. Mama's candle grew brighter as we walked.

Rosco and I each drifted into our own private thoughts. I was still itching to know more letters, but the two that I had just learned were enough to ring inside me like a happy little play-song: *P-Q-P* . . . *Q-P-Q* . . . *P-Q-P* . . .

6

ROSCO

September 11, 1862

IT WAS GONNA TAKE A MIRACLE to teach Summer to read. She was so eager to get letters and words in her head all at once that she wasn't paying full attention, and she wasn't learning nothin'. If she wasn't my sister, I'd have told her that I didn't have no time to waste trying to teach an addle-head.

And Summer talked way too much. After our lesson, soon as we got back to the quarters, she was all set to start bragging to Mama about her *Q*'s and *P*'s. She was ready to announce to every slave on Parnell's place that I was giving her book lessons. But I shushed her with a single cut of my eyes, and she swallowed back her excitement. It was a good thing I had taken her book from her. She'd have been waving it right up under Master Gideon's nose if I'd let her keep it. My backbone went cold just to think about the trouble Summer could have brought with her restlessness.

This morning I was at the blacksmith shack with Clem, helping him keep the irons' fire alive. "You know anything 'bout coloreds fighting in the war?" I asked cautiously.

Clem looked at me sideways. "Maybe so, maybe not," was all he said. Clem was good at not letting on that he had know-how about certain things. When he didn't want to let go of what he knew, he said stuff like, "Could be." Or, "It's possible." Or, "That's a question for the heavens." Sometimes, Clem didn't answer at all; he just shrugged. That's when I knew to back away from badgering him.

But when Clem answered me with a "Could be," or an "It's possible," it was because he wanted to see how much *I* knew before he committed himself to sharing any information he had tucked in his back pocket.

Clem hadn't always been as short on words as he was now. Just last summer he was serious in love with Marietta, a girl who lived nearby on the Johnston plantation. I never saw a man more giddy than Clem when Marietta came to Parnell's with her mistress to visit Missy Claire. Clem even got dreamy-eyed when he *talked* 'bout Marietta (and he talked 'bout her—'bout her pretty honey-colored skin and her true understanding of how to grow flowers and harvest berries—all the time). Talked about Marietta like she was some kind of queen. He even used to call her Queen Etta, a nickname he let roll off his lips every chance he got. Heck, whenever I was fetching water from Parnell's well, I secretly wished that when I got to be Clem's age—he was sixteen, three years more than me—I'd be lucky enough to find me a Marietta of my own.

It didn't take long for Marietta and Clem to decide they were truly matched in the eyes of God. But they wanted to make their match official, so Clem went to Master Gideon and asked to get hitched. He asked if Parnell would purchase Marietta, so's the two of them could live together as husband and wife.

I wasn't there when Clem asked to marry, of course, but I hear tell that Parnell didn't even consider it. He said no almost before Clem got the words out.

Gideon is said to have told Clem, "I got enough womenfolk among my slaves."

Clem said the master told him to "tie the knot with one of the fine women right here on this plantation. I'll bless any marriage that's between two of my own slaves."

But Clem didn't want one of Parnell's slaves. He wanted Marietta. Back then, Clem was strong-willed, and when something didn't sit right with him, he spoke his mind about it. But rather than go at the master in his haughty way, people say he got real humble, and he begged the master to buy Marietta so's they could marry. He told Parnell about all the things Marietta could bring to his plantation—how she would make Missy Claire's flower beds the envy of everybody in Hobbs Hollow. And how she could harvest some of the healthiest vegetables anywhere.

Clem's persistence didn't pay off. The master said no, and he meant it.

That same night, Clem and Marietta ran off. It was the second full moon in August, to be exact. I remember, 'cause Thea still spoke on it long after it happened, said all kinds of hexes happened under a full moon, that a second full moon in the same month made any hexes double, and that Clem and Marietta should have waited till the moon was new before they fled.

I sure wish Clem had told me he was plannin' to run. I could have slowed up Marlon, the master's horse, by overfeeding him. And I could have mixed some bad meat into the food barrel of Parnell's search dogs, so's they'd be too sick to hunt.

Master Gideon didn't waste no time calling on the bounty-fetchers to find Clem, 'cause Clem was valuable to him. He was the slave who knew how to best tend horses, pigs, and dogs.

Marietta and Clem were caught just beyond the back woods of Parnell's property, at Holly Glen, not too far north of Hobbs Hollow. Master Gideon's dogs sniffed them out in no time.

Marietta, she was sold off to cotton country, to the

deep south of Mississippi, where the slave masters were meaner than the devil himself. Clem, he was brought back here and whipped somethin' awful. But it wasn't Master Gideon who whipped him. I never saw that man lift a whip. He never carried out whippings. He *couldn't*. Whipping wasn't in him.

Even though Parnell said he believed runnin' off was grounds for a whippin', I didn't think he fully believed it. Seems he wanted to show his town council buddies that he was up to punishing nigras. So whenever the situation called for it, Gideon made Rance, his overseer, do the dirty work. "*Carry it out*," was what he said when they brought Clem back. And after he gave the order, he disappeared—never stood by to watch his slaves get beat.

I seen a few real bad whippings, but I will never forget the day Rance Smalley put the whip to my friend Clem. Thea says it was hell come to earth.

Sometimes when I closed my eyes at night, I could still see that whippin', like it happened yesterday. Remembering it was as bad as ten demon dreams rolled into one. (And it often led to a night of haints stealing my sleep.)

Even when I thought on that whippin' when I was wide awake, I saw it clear as day. Clem bleeding, all 'cross his shoulders and down his back. Rance's bullwhip hurling forward, snapping in the air, like a wild, dancing snake, then landing on Clem's flesh with a loud, stinging slap.

I remembered the grimace on Clem's face, too. His teeth gritted, his jaw tight. But more than anything, I remember that when Rance was flinging his whip, Clem was stone-silent. He didn't holler, or cry out, or nothin'. And after the whippin' was done—after Rance had gone and left Clem hanging, and Thea and Mama had untied Clem's wrists from the branches of Parnell's old hickory tree—Clem still didn't utter a single sound. Not a cry, or a whimper even.

Weeks later, when Clem had healed some (it took days and nights of Thea and Mama dressing Clem's wounds with root salves), Clem was different. Strange-different. It was like he'd lost the will to speak. He'd gone silent, with just a little bit of talking here and there.

Still, since Clem and me were friends, I could get him to speaking more than other folks could. He talked to me more than he talked to anybody. We were still at the blacksmith shack when I floated my question past him again, hoping maybe he'd give me more of an answer this time. "You know anything 'bout coloreds fighting in the war?"

Clem was slow to speak, but I could tell by the way his eyes shifted that he was quickly mulling over his thoughts. He positioned a stick of hot iron onto his anvil and began to pound it into a horseshoe. "Why you keep askin'?" His eyes stayed on his work.

I lowered my voice. "I hear the Union army has let in colored fighters."

Clem cooled his smoldering horseshoe in the water barrel next to his anvil.

"I'm thinking of enlisting," I whispered, "but I don't know how."

Clem's face went tight, but he was looking right at me when he said, "I know how."

7
Summer
September 14, 1862

HOT DAYS MADE ME squirrely. Made me want to run and jump and play. And these had been some of the hottest days ever on the Parnell plantation. Come lately, all I could think about was two things: cooling my toes in the stream over by the meadow, and learning my letters.

I had a hard time keeping the chitty-chat quiet in my head—my thoughts flipped round like a trapped crab—while I helped Thea beat the parlor rugs. We were preparing the house for Missy Claire's social, which she held each month. Mama was making tea cakes for the occasion. I could smell their sweetness rising from the cookhouse oven.

Missy Claire's monthly gathering of women from the Hobbs Hollow Arts and Letters Society was something I dreaded. When it came to having visitors, Missy Claire got to be nitpicky 'bout every little thing. And since Mama ran things in the Parnell cookhouse, she got the worst of Missy's persnickety ways. This morning she was lording over Mama. I could hear her voice flying up between Mama's humming.

"*Kit*, don't forget to arrange the cakes as I prefer—stacked like a petticoat."

"*Kit*, you got the china ready?"

"Make sure I can see my reflection in the silver, *Kit*."

Thea huffed a short breath, the kind that chases away a fly. "This rug's got it easier than your mama," she whispered, picking at a natty tuft of lint that had clustered at the rug's edge.

Every time Missy Claire had her society meeting, she swore it was "fresh water for the flowers of the soul." But from what I had seen, the meeting wasn't nothing more than Missy Claire, Penelope Bates, the doctor's wife, and Amelia Tucker, mistress of the Tucker-Wilkes plantation, talking proper, and finishing off Mama's tea cakes.

And now that I knew me two letters—two letters of the alphabet—I also knew I had never seen or heard the ladies from the Hobbs Hollow Arts and Letters Society talk nothing 'bout no letters—at least not the way Rosco talked about them.

I wasn't sure what *arts* was. Maybe arts was eating tea

cakes, and maybe filling your belly with them made learning letters easier.

Thea once told me that Missy Claire's socials had little to do with watering any kind of flowers—for the soul or otherwise. She said them meetings were more for keeping Missy Claire's mind off Lowell's bad lungs.

Along with being a seer, Thea was the one who birthed babies. She birthed me and Rosco, and she even birthed young Master Lowell. I once heard her telling Mama that Missy Claire had it hard when Lowell was pushing his way into this world. "She was screaming all out her head, and cursin' her own womanhood," Thea said.

Lowell's coming was hard on Missy Claire. Thea says that when Lowell was born, she was the one who had to tell Master Gideon that Missy Claire wouldn't be able to have no more babies. But when she told the master he had himself a son, he didn't care a hoot about more young'uns. Thea says he just kept saying, "Lowell Farnsworth Parnell, the pride of the Parnell legacy."

But as soon as Master Gideon found out his "*Parnell legacy*" had clouded lungs—Thea says she knew the boy was sickly right when he let out his first cry—Parnell shunned both little baby Lowell and Missy Claire. Thea once said, "He acts like the two of them have wronged him unforgivably."

I tried to be mindful of Missy Claire's hardship. I

tried to look upon her with eyes of kindness, like Mama told me to. But it was hard sometimes, especially on days like this when Missy Claire's parlor rug—the biggest in the Parnell home—was spread out before me like an unpicked cotton field.

Thea and me, we had our own way of cleaning Missy Claire's rug. We'd come up with what Thea liked to say was "a way of beatin' the beast."

Thea hung the rug over the porch railing—it spread the whole length of the rail, and fell all the way to the bushes that marked the entryway to the house—then she and I leaned over the rail and beat the rug from the top.

My shoulders had begun to ache from swinging my wipplestick, the long-handled paddle we used to pound the rugs free of their dust. Every time I stopped to rub the cramp from my hands, Thea said, "The more you rest, the longer we got 'fore we done."

That's when I came up with my own special way of making the work go quicker. I started in with my play-song, slow at first, then fast: "*P-Q-P . . . Q-P-Q . . . P-Q-P.*"

Thea threw me a solid look. "What's that you singing, child?" She was shading her eyes from the sun, and frowning. There was concern clouding her eyes and a knowing expression coming to her face at the same time.

I knew right then that I shouldn't have been singing about them letters I learned from Rosco. "I was just making me up a ditty," I said, swallowing hard.

Thea set down her wipplestick. "*What* ditty?"

I was beating on the rug real hard now. My eyes avoided Thea's. I tried to make like I didn't hear Thea's asking, but she pressed me with another question that I just couldn't ignore. She said it more like an answer than a question. Her voice was low as a whisper when she spoke. "You learnin' letters, aren't you."

I shrugged.

Thea rested her hand on one hip. She stood there looking at me straight, waiting for me to say something.

I nodded.

"Rosco," Thea said simply.

I nodded again.

"It's hard to keep in, ain't it? Feels good to let out what you know, don't it?" Thea was still whispering. Whispering with her whole mouth, enough to show off her dark gums and twisted teeth.

I nodded a third time.

"I know me plenty, but I can't go shoutin' it to the world, Summer," Thea said softly. "And neither can you."

After that I didn't utter a single *Q* or a *P*, or not much else, for that matter. Thea and I just kept on beating Missy Claire's rug till every speck of dust had risen from its fibers.

Later, at the quarters, Thea called me off to the cypress tree, the same tree where Rosco and me had our first lesson.

"Summer"—she was measuring her words—"learning

letters is a boon and a bugaboo, all rolled into one. It's good, and it's bad, at the same time."

Thea wasn't talking like she was mad, but something in me felt like I was being scolded. I pinched the fabric of my dress and let Thea go on.

"If folks ever get wind that you or Rosco got even an inkling to read—"

Thea was telling me what Mama had already said. "Then I'll be sold off, or worse," I interrupted.

Thea peered at me sharply. "You sassin' me, Summer?"

I lowered my eyes. "No," I said softly. "It's just that even the few letters I know—the *P* and the *Q*—and the others I seen in the book Rosco gave me for my birthday, well, they make me feel so good when I look at 'em. They're like tiny dancers, Thea, bending and stretching, right on the page." Tears started to tug at my throat. It was as if Thea were snatching my book right out from me. But I didn't want to let it go.

She cupped her palm to my cheek. "Everybody's got a silent thunder, child, and I can see you've found yours."

I didn't know what Thea meant, but I sure wasn't gonna interrupt her again. So I let her speak on.

"Silent thunder is desire, longing," Thea explained. "You can't hear it, or see it, but you can sure *feel* it, roaring up in you, calling you ahead. It's when you want something so bad that even your bones know it."

I was nodding fast at Thea's words. She was describing what I was feeling each time I even *thought* about learning to read. And now I had the words for it: *Silent thunder.*

"Rosco's got his own silent thunder raging up in him," Thea said. "I pray it don't push him to do something foolish, the way it did with Clem."

"Rosco's got a love?" I asked.

"Yes, Summer, Rosco has himself a deep-down hankering, but it's not a girl. It's a different kind of passion that's driving that boy."

"It's his reading, ain't it?" I figured.

Thea nodded. "That's only a piece of it. The rest ain't for you to know. I'm only tellin' you so's you understand that every soul—a man's, a woman's, your very own brother's—carries some kind of silent thunder. But listen, silent thunder is something we got to keep quiet and private." Thea let go a slow breath. "That's the way of slavery, Summer," she said. "Anything that makes you feel good has gotta stay cooped up, like a toad wriggling inside a croaker sack, else it can be taken away."

I let all that Thea was telling me settle still for a moment. Then I asked, "Mama's got a silent thunder?"

Thea nodded. "She does."

"You got it, too?"

"Yes, Summer."

Now I was thinking hard on what Thea had been saying. "Rosco told you 'bout his thunder?" I asked.

Thea shook her head. "He doesn't need to speak on it."

"Then how do you know, Thea?"

"That's what a seer is, child," she said. "I can see silent thunder happening in people." Thea sighed. "And just like your learning letters," she said, "seeing into people is a boon and a bugaboo."

8

Rosco

September 22, 1862

"Announced by all the trumpets of the sky,
Arrives the snow, and, driving o'er the fields,
Seems nowhere to alight: the whited air
Hides hills and woods, the river, and the heaven,
And veils the farm-house at the garden's end. . . ."

I WAS POLISHING THE DOORKNOBS just outside Master Gideon's study, listening to Lowell finishing up his lesson.

My thoughts were clouded. Clouded with what Clem had told me at the smithing shack. From that day to this, it seemed all's I could think on was enlisting in the Union army.

But when I heard Lowell reading aloud for Miss McCracken, my thoughts turned to the beauty of poetry, which Lowell was reading without a single snag. His voice was soft and even, and he put weight to certain words to bring the poem alive—*snow, heaven, veils, garden's end* . . .

When I peeked through the half-open doorway, Miss McCracken was looking on approvingly. "Very good reading, Lowell," she said as Lowell's eyes rose from his book. "Ralph Waldo Emerson's 'The Snow-Storm,' a lovely poem by one of our finest."

Lowell coughed from deep down. "Yes—ma'am." Now he was back to stuttering, like somebody had snatched his voice right out of him.

"That'll be enough for today," Miss McCracken said, settling her hand on Lowell's bony shoulder. Lowell sat back from his book and nodded.

Miss McCracken's eyes met mine as she left the study. There was kindness in her eyes, kindness in her whole face. Miss McCracken never let a lesson pass when she didn't regard me with some goodly gesture, usually a brief nod of her head and a tiny smile. (And I never let a single lesson pass when I wasn't close by to receive her courtesy.)

Rose McCracken's name fit her rightly, on account of her pink skin. She and I never spoke a word to each other, but whenever she looked at me and gave me her quick, single nod, her eyes seemed to be saying, "*Rosco, you're as good as anybody else, nothing low about you.*"

Of course, I didn't dare hold Miss McCracken's gaze long enough to see if she was telling me anything else. It wouldn't be proper for me to rest my eyes on hers for more than a moment. And today, like all days, I looked to the floorboards as soon as Miss McCracken graced me with her brief bit of politeness.

I tried to keep my attention to polishing the doorknob, but I couldn't help but listen to the rustle made by Miss McCracken's skirts as she walked down the dirt entry road that snaked onto Parnell's plantation. The gentle swish of her dress carried the same dignity she did. When I couldn't hear the brush of her steps anymore, I knew she was truly gone for the day, and something in me sunk.

Lowell went back to reading aloud from his lesson book:

"Announced by all the trumpets of the sky,
Arrives the snow, and, driving o'er the fields. . . ."

In the years I been listening in on Lowell's lessons, I ain't never heard him read out loud after his lesson was over.

Right then, he read real smooth—not even a break to his voice.

"Seems nowhere to alight: the whited air
Hides hills and woods, the river, and the heaven,"

I stopped my polishing so's I could listen.

Forgetting myself, I stood full-well in the doorway to the study, my cleaning rag dangling from my hand, watching Lowell read the poem like he was delivering an announcement to the state.

After Lowell spoke the final line—*"And veils the farmhouse at the garden's end"*—he looked right at me. I blinked, but I kept my eyes with his.

Then, Lowell motioned me to him.

I hesitated. "Master Lowell?"

He gestured again. "Come see," he said softly, tilting his book toward me.

I could feel the skin moisten above my lip. The backs of my ears went hot. "I best keep with the doorknob," I said, lowering my eyes.

Lowell let out a tiny cough. He said, "I've seen how you listen close when Miss McCracken and I do our lessons."

I tried to swallow the dry patch that had settled at the back of my throat. I shrugged.

Lowell was smoothing his hand over the page of his book as if it were a tiny kitten. Even in the dim room, I could see the page's creamy softness, cradling its beautiful poem-words. Words that I wanted to see up close, but couldn't. My mind raced with wondering how I could swipe that book, same way as I'd swiped *The Clarkston Reader*. I wondered how I could take Emerson's "Snow-Storm" for a day so's I could see Lowell's poem for myself. So's I could make it *my* poem. So's I could put *my* voice to its pretty words.

Now I was polishing hard on the doorknob. I was trying to pretend Lowell had never spoken to me. But Lowell wouldn't give up. He took a weighty breath. Then he began to stutter. "Come on, Rosco. Come s-s-s-ee my book," he repeated.

I shook my head. "Can't, Master Lowell—can't," I said firmly.

I couldn't help but wonder why, all 'a sudden, Lowell was inviting me to see his lesson book. There had to be something more to it, and as badly as I wanted to set my eyes on *"all the trumpets of the sky,"* I couldn't take me no chances—not a one. I couldn't help but wonder, though: Did Lowell know I'd learned me to read?

I cut my eyes toward Lowell's to see if I could read his intentions. But all's I saw on his face was pleading. Lowell truly wanted me to look at the poem along with him, and I, for the living gizzards of me, couldn't figure out why.

One thing was for certain, though. It was the thing I knew as sure as I knew my name was Rosco Parnell. That snowstorm Lowell was reading 'bout in that poem would have to fall all over the devil's hell before he or any white man ever roped me into showing I could read, or ever tried to pry the power of reading from me.

Finally, seeing that I was set on ignoring him, Lowell gave up. He closed his lesson book and hugged it to his chest. He left me to my doorknob, which was now shiny enough for me to see the reflection of my own troubled frown.

9
Summer
September 28, 1862

ON SUNDAY MORNING I WOKE again before the sun had even thought of rising. Woke shortly after Mama woke. *Early.*

Mama always left the quarters before anybody, when the sky was still black, with not even a hint of morning light. She often said, "Gotta fill the house with the smell of breakfast, while the Parnells is still 'sleep. And if it's Sunday, gotta fill it good. Gideon won't stand for meeting the dawn without my biscuits and gravy calling his name. And Missy, well, you know how she likes her hair done up pretty for church."

Mama put her head to her pallet every night, but I wondered if she ever really slept. Seemed all she ever did was work. That's why it wasn't often that I saw Mama dress for the day.

But today was different.

Mama had lit her lantern, like always (even when she had the lantern lighted, I was usually 'sleep). She didn't know I'd woken up. For a moment, I kept my eyes closed to slits, enough to stay like I was 'sleep, but to enjoy the early hours of waking, too.

Mama rose from her pallet. With her back partly to me—I opened my eyes fully when Mama got to be busy with getting herself ready to go to the Parnells' kitchen—I watched her slip out of her night frock. That's when I saw it, plain as the day that would be coming on. Mama's scar—her brand. The letter *P*, burned deep into her hip, same way as it was on Rosco and on me. But Mama's scar was even more puckered. Even more blackened. It was truly ugly.

I squeezed my eyes shut. There was nothing more for me to see. Still, though, I could feel my eyes dancing under their lids. While I listened to Mama rustle quietly in the dim glow of her lantern, I slid my hand to my own brand. Over and over, I traced my finger around the *P*'s hump. Soon I could feel my fingers start to tremble. Then a tug closed off my throat. Next thing I knew, I had wet coming to my eyes. And just as my tears started to spill, Mama slid from the quarters, leaving me to weep silently in the dark.

It was still twilight when Rosco and I met up on the dirt path that lead to the house. Rosco was on his way to tend to Lowell's morning—helping Lowell rise, having the basin wash-water ready, and making sure his church clothes were set for the day.

I was on my way to work 'longside Mama in the cookhouse. The sight of Mama's scar hadn't left me. I still had tears snatching at my insides. I was trying real hard to think of other things—to shake the memory, same way I shake the wrinkles from Missy Claire's table linens—but, deep down, I had a feeling this morning's sight would stay in my thoughts for a long time coming.

As soon as Rosco and I started walking, Rosco reached in his back pocket and pulled out something that looked like one of Thea's herb pouches, the kind she presses on bruises and wounds to help them heal.

"Here, Summer," he said, pushing the pouch into my chest. "It's a present."

I held the pouch over toward Rosco's lantern. "My birthday's been come and gone for weeks now," I said, turning over the funny-looking pouch.

"Think of it as an any-ol'-time present," Rosco said. "I made it for you, Summer. Stuffed and sewed it myself. It's a dolly."

I looked at Rosco sidelong. "Since when did *you* know how to sew?" I asked.

"Since I got me the feeling to make you that dolly."

Behind us, we could hear the field slaves beginning to spread through the tobacco fields, ready for another long day of picking. Rosco motioned to me. "We better not dawdle," he said. "Gideon can be real cranky on Sundays. Mama says it's 'cause he hates going to church." Rosco had walked a few steps ahead. I trailed not far behind as he spoke. "Missy Claire makes Parnell sit in the front pew every week. He sure don't like doin' that, and it's worse when Lowell gets to stuttering his way through the prayers and hymns. That shames Parnell bad, Mama says." Rosco was picking up his pace. I had to walk double time to keep up. "Master Gideon won't take kindly to us being late," he said.

The doll Rosco made me was far from pretty, not like them china-head dolls Missy Claire's got sitting up on her bed pillows. (Them's the dolls Missy's had since she was a child herself, Mama says.)

Rosco's handmade dolly wasn't no more than a scrap of burlap from some old flour sack, stuffed with a hump of cotton. Its arms and legs were spruce twigs hitched to the doll's body so's they could move.

And that thing wore the funniest little face. A face made from a walnut shell. Its face looked wrinkly, like Thea's face is starting to look. Wrinkly, but wise, somehow. And the doll's walnut face was the same color brown as Mama's face, and my face, too.

"What's her name?" I asked, bringing the dolly's skinny twig-arms together and out again, helping her do a hand clap.

"Name her what you want." Rosco shrugged.

"How 'bout I name her Walnut, like her face."

Rosco shook his head, like he was feeling sorry 'bout something. "I wish I could'a got you a china-face dolly, Summer, the kind they make for white girls."

I was thinking the same thing, but there was a hint of regret in Rosco's eyes that kept me from saying what was on my mind. Walnut was far from china. Real far. I tried to make Rosco feel better by telling him something I didn't truly believe. "Them china dolls is too flimsy, anyhow. They break quick as an egg if you drop one. Heck, Walnut here, she's special. You could drop her a million times over and she'd still be good as new."

Now Rosco was looking sidelong at me. "You expect me to believe you're really thinking that's true, Summer?"

I shook my head. I let go a tiny smile. "Can't blame me for trying, Ros." I walked Walnut's spindly legs out in front of me as if she were walking on the air, walking along with us. "Why'd you make me this doll, anyhow, Ros?" I asked. "This any-ol'-time present?"

"You need a friend you can talk to in private—any ol' time. Somebody who ain't got ears for hearing, a mouth for talking back, or the ways of a seer," Rosco said.

As we approached the house, I could see the light of Mama's lantern coming from the cookhouse.

Rosco put a firm hand on my shoulder. "Thea told me how you were spouting them letters I taught you— the P and the Q." He gave me a solid look. "You can't be doing that, Summer."

"I can't help it, Ros," I said. "I got what Thea says is—"

"I know, Summer. I know about the silent thunder," he interrupted. "I got it too," he said softly. "But I don't go *telling* everybody." Rosco pointed toward Walnut with his chin. "I sewed you the dolly so's you can tell *her* all I been teaching you. So's you can let your cat out of the bag in a way that won't cause no trouble."

Now I was holding Walnut to me. She was starting to feel like a friend already. "How do you mean?" I wanted to know.

Rosco gently lifted Walnut from my hold. "Like this," he said, whispering close to the side of Walnut's tiny head.

"Looks like you're saying a prayer to her."

"I'm prayin' all right," Rosco said. "Prayin' you get knocked with some horse sense." Rosco's lips were still pressed close to the place where Walnut's ear would be if she were a china doll. "I'm showing you how it is you should tell this here dolly what you know," Rosco said. "Speak to her more quiet than the breeze speaks to the sky. If you do that, Summer, you can speak as much of your mind as you please."

I had to think on that for a moment. "Can I tell her when I'm feeling squirrely?"

Rosco nodded.

"Can I tell her what I think 'bout Missy Claire and her Arts and Letters Society?"

Rosco nodded again. "You can tell her any deep-down thing you want."

"I got a lot I want to tell Walnut," I said quietly.

"Good," Rosco encouraged. "'Long as you say it so's only *she* can hear. Promise me, Summer."

"I promise."

Rosco gave my hand a little squeeze.

"Ros," I asked, "what *is* arts, anyway?"

Rosco thought a moment. "Arts is a special way of doing something, making something fine as can be. Like Mama's way of shaping tea cakes. And Clem's way of shoeing horses. That's arts," Rosco said.

We were at the front steps of the house now, about to go inside, about to face our work for the day.

But I was too squirrely to work. I twirled Walnut by her arms. Spun her out in front of me to make her dance. Then, like a cricket springing free from under a leaf, I asked Rosco, "You ever wonder why we ain't got no pa?"

"Everybody's got a pa."

I went back to cuddling my dolly. "Who's our pa, then?"

Rosco's jaw went tight. "Somebody," was all he said.

"Somebody who? And where's he at?"

Rosco kicked at the steps in front of him. "Girl, you always got a bees' nest of questions buzzing up in you. It's enough to drive a good man to agitation."

I could smell Mama's biscuits. "You ever ask Mama 'bout our daddy?"

Rosco kicked at the steps again, harder this time. "Nope," he said.

"How come?"

Rosco wouldn't look at me then. He said, "Half the slaves on this place don't know nothin' about who their pa is."

"But don't you ever wonder, Ros?"

Now Rosco's jaw was tight as ever. "I ain't like you, Summer. I ain't got the same bees bothering me. I don't *want* to know the answer to every last little thing."

"But this ain't little, Ros."

Rosco went around to the side door of the house. Before he walked up the back steps to Lowell's room, he said, "Summer, if you mess with too many bees, you come away with a bad sting."

I cradled Walnut, listening to Rosco creak his way up the stairs, wishing I'd remembered to ask him about his own silent thunder.

10

ROSCO

September 28, 1862

I LOVED SUNDAY MORNINGS at the house, when the Parnells had gone to church. It was quiet, and I could take a moment to watch the sun stretch its arms along the walls of the master's study.

Today, lady sun was doing a fine job dancing across Master Parnell's writing desk. And she did me a true favor by calling my attention to the *Harper's Weekly* that was folded open and resting on the desk blotter.

I leaned over the desk, just enough to see a headline and a good bit of the main story. My eyes followed down the page. I spotted President Abraham Lincoln's name right away. Then I came to two words I didn't know. Two long words I tried to sound out silently.

Emancipation Proclamation.

The article said the president had presented a draft of this Emancipation Proclamation to Congress, and

that he intended to issue a formal version of the document at the first of the new year, 1863. This document
would call for the freedom of all slaves.

Right then, something flinched inside my chest. I
read the final sentence again, letting my eyes rest on
each word. I had to make sure I was reading them right.

I got a little hum up inside me; a strange, eager feeling. The same excitement I got whenever I rode Dash at
a sprint in the far meadow. It was a feeling I didn't fully
understand, but I sure liked the way it swelled in my
belly. I had to will my insides to be still.

The freedom of all slaves.

Them words were easy. I didn't even need to sound
them out.

But the longer words—*Emancipation Proclamation*—still
snagged in my throat. They were the kind of words that
set me a challenge. A challenge that wouldn't let me step
away without giving it a good go.

I sounded them two long-lettered words over and
over till I could hear myself pronouncing them out-
right. When I spoke the words slowly, I could feel my
lips and tongue get a hold of them.

Emancipation Proclamation.

Soon I was reading them words smooth as butter,
reading them like they were a song, almost.

That's when I heard Mama calling my name.

She was hollering full-out, scared and shaky. A holler
I ain't never heard come from Mama. "*Rosco!*"

I quickly put the *Harper's Weekly* back like I'd found it and hurried to the front entry, where Mama and Clem were hoisting Master Gideon off the drive-seat of his carriage. Summer stood by, holding Walnut close to her chest. Missy Claire and Lowell were still inside the carriage. Missy's shoulders were curled in around her. Her whole face was buried in both hands. Lowell was carefully lifting pieces of hair away from his mother's cupped fingers.

Thea came running from the well at the side of the house, holding a dipper of water. Clem and Mama set Master Gideon out on the grass beside the entry road. He lay flat on his back, his belly sagging. He was bloated and babbling things none of us could understand. His eyelids fluttered when he tried to speak.

Thea knelt beside him. She lifted his head, parted his lips, and tried to help him take in some water. But it was no use. The master couldn't drink. The water spilled from the sides of his mouth and dribbled down his front.

Thea looked from Clem to Mama to me. Worry clenched her face. "Want me to bring some cayenne liniment?" I asked Mama.

Mama shook her head once. "No, child," she said, "liniment won't help this."

11
Summer
September 29, 1862

YESTERDAY, WHEN THE PARNELLS came home from church, the master was in an awful way. Somethin' bad had happened to him. Somethin' I ain't never seen or known about. The master's body was two ways at once: limp as gooseflesh, and stiff as a barn door. I would've sworn the master was dead, with the way Mama and Clem had him laid out on the grass.

But Parnell didn't look as though he was gonna let anything or anybody take him from this life. Even in his helplessness, he wore a stubborn expression.

He was talkin' gibberish. But if I'd had a cent to my name, I'd have bet he was giving an order—*"Leave me alone."*

At Mama's insistence, Rosco loosened the cravat that had become twisted at the master's neck. The master's pits and front were soaked with sweat. That's how I truly knew that he was nowhere near dead. I ain't never known a dead person to speak or sweat or protest the way Gideon Parnell was doin' under the high afternoon sun.

Soon after, Doc Bates rushed up in his wagon. He pressed his fingers to the spot where Master Gideon's ear meets his neck and, right then, the doctor told us all who were standing there that the master had suffered "an apoplectic stroke." Doc said he'd only seen a few cases of what he called "apoplexy," and that we could expect the master to "wither in his limbs" and "lose the abilities of articulation."

Them words didn't mean nothing to me when Doc Bates said them. But I knew by the way Missy Claire was shuddering and choking on her tears that what the master had was a real bad thing. And I heard her tell Doc Bates that Gideon's own pa had suffered something similar, before he'd died and left the Parnell plantation to Gideon.

That night, back at the quarters, everybody had something to say about Master Gideon's stroke—about what was really wrong with him (some disagreed with Doc Bates's call), and about how we'd all fare now that the master was too sick to run his plantation.

A small group sat around the table and argued. Each person seemed stuck in his or her own belief. And all of us seemed agitated about the day's happenings.

Thea said Master Gideon had been cursed with

what she called "heart-shock," a wicked condition that didn't sound too far off from Doc Bates's description. She explained that one of Master Gideon's hands and arms and maybe even one of his legs would shrivel and wither like a dead fish. And, Thea told us, Gideon Parnell would come to speak like the sloppy drunks that stagger around the town alleys at odd hours of the night. And that his speech would turn to slur forever, without him even taking a drop of whisky.

Thea spoke with true authority, even more than Doc Bates had. We all listened close, and nobody disagreed. While Thea spoke, I could see Mama's lips reciting a prayer.

All the slaves on Parnell's place stayed up later than usual that night. It was the men, mostly, who sat up debating about what would happen now. I saw Rosco and Clem swapping glances. Me, I held Walnut tighter than ever.

"Missy Claire sure can't run things," said Eagan, Parnell's oldest field slave.

Pippin, who mans the smokehouse, said, "Parnell's boy, that sickly runt of a child, don't have nowhere near what it takes to step into his daddy's shoes."

Clem stood up when he spoke. He said, "This whole thing is a dream come true for Rance Smalley, Parnell's overseer."

Everybody listened close to Clem, who was talking

in a fury. "You know what they say: 'When the cat's away, the mice will play.' And Rance is gonna use this as *his* chance to play—to play like he's the boss man. Remember how it was whenever Parnell went to Charlottesville for an overnight visit? Rance loved to act like this plantation was all his."

A few of the men piped up. They were agreeing with Clem.

Mama shushed everybody. "Let's not jump to all kinds of notions."

Then Rosco spoke up. "I got me a bit of hearsay," he said. He looked from me to Mama to Clem. "I got wind that freedom's comin'," he said softly.

Several men pulled their chairs closer to the table. "Speak on it. What's the hearsay?" Pippin gave Rosco a nudge.

I saw Mama listening as close as the men.

Rosco licked his lips. "I hear our very own president has written up a freedom paper." Now Rosco's eyes took a moment to look at each and every one of us as he spoke. "He's puttin' together what folks is calling a 'proclamation'—an order that will set us all free, come the new year."

Some of the men laughed. "Boy, you been hearin' tall tales," said Eagan.

Clem, who was still standing, sat down sharply. "Where you been gettin' this hearsay, Rosco?"

Rosco was slow to answer. Some of the men leaned

in toward Rosco. Finally Rosco said, "I get hearsay same way as anybody else: from keeping my ears cocked and my eyes open."

Late into the night, when Mama and me finally settled onto our pallets, I took comfort in Walnut's tiny brown body and in my *Clarkston Reader*. I kept my lantern burning low, close to my pallet, so's I could see my book.

That's when, all of a sudden, Mama scolded me. "Snuff that lantern, child—snuff it now. And put that wretched foolishness away, you hear." Mama was whispering with a sure force. Even in the dimness, I could see her anger.

I knew arguing was no use, though I tried. "But Mama, I'm—"

"Don't give me sass, Summer," she snapped. "I'm a tired woman tonight. We've had enough bad fortune come to this plantation for one day, and we don't need no more. I told you to keep that book hid away, and I told Rosco the same about any books he gets his hands on. But Rosco, he ain't like you—he knows better than to be waving a stolen book around."

I wanted to tell Mama that I had me a silent thunder, and that everyone—even her—had one, too. And that letters were beautiful, fancy things. But Mama wasn't hearing me, not tonight. I slid my book closer to me. "Mama, I'm not *waving* it around," I said.

But faster than I could blink, Mama snatched the book from my hands. Thankfully, none of the pages tore, though something inside me was ripping fast. Mama spoke her final words. "Child, this is the *wrong* night for talkin' back to your mama. This blasted book is gonna stay with me from here on. You ain't got no more use for it."

"I *do* have use for it!" I snapped. "Why you gotta take it *now?*"

Mama spoke firmly. "I'm takin' it *now* so's we don't risk any trouble from here on in. With Gideon's heart-shock, there's gonna be all kinds of white folks comin' round here. Surely, we'll have visitors—friends of the Parnells—and just plain nosy people from town who want to see for themselves what's happening now that Gideon's sickly. This plantation is gonna be swarming with white folks soon as tomorrow. The last thing I need is for you to go around flauntin' a book."

I was too churned up to speak. When I parted my lips to say something, to give Mama more of my protest, not even the squeak of a mouse came to my throat. But Mama must have seen the disappointment on my face. She said, "Wipe that pout off your lips and listen to me good. If I find you dabbling with letters again, I'll give you a true reason to be down in the mouth."

I snuffed my lantern. I rolled to my side. I whispered to Walnut way into the darkness.

PART TWO

Serendipity

12

ROSCO

October 28, 1862

MAMA'S CRADLING A TINY BABY. I can see his little body wriggling in Mama's arms as she lets droplets of sugar-water drip from her finger onto the baby's suckling lips.

The baby lets out a whimper. Mama rocks him, coos down into the blanket, where he's bundled tight. That baby's whimper sets something off in me. Makes me want to cuddle that babe in my own arms. "Can I hold him, Mama?"

Mama shakes her head. "Best that I tend to him," she says. "But come, take a look." Mama loosens the blanket where it's tucked at the baby's chin. She peels the soft fabric away from the baby's face.

Soon as I peer in, I'm startled back. This baby's got the face of a grown man. The face of Gideon Parnell!

Mama doesn't see what I see. To her, there ain't nothin' strange about the baby. She coddles him. Strokes his face gently. Wipes the spittle from his chin.

I look closer to make sure my eyes aren't playing a trick on me.

I turn back the blanket so's I can see even more of the baby. On the place where that baby's ribs would be, there's a fleshy, pink wound—a cattle brand, like the one me and Summer and Mama and all of us Parnell slaves got burned into our sides. But this half baby—half Gideon isn't branded with the letter P. *He's got Mama's name—Kit—burned into him. And the brand is surrounded by the black body hairs of a full-grown man! I shudder and wince at the same time.*

Mama don't notice the baby's brand, either. This baby is all sweetness to her. She folds his blanket back around him, double-checking to make sure he's properly wrapped.

Then something happens to make me holler. Mama and her baby rise from the land and float up toward the sky. Same way seed pods rise from a dandelion. The two of them are floating fast and far. Soon they grow smaller and smaller among the clouds. With a breeze blowing at them, Mama's dress billows up to reveal the brand on her thigh. I look away from shame, from not wanting to see my own mama's bare legs. I'm calling out, "Mama, Mama!" until I realize that I'm not dreaming no more, that I'm coming to wakefulness.

My eyes flew open. Twilight was creeping. "Mama's left for the main house," Summer said in a sleepy voice. "You all right, Ros?"

"It ain't nothin'," I said. "Just askin' for Mama, is all."

But this time, Mama wasn't there to chase away the haints in my dream. So I found comfort in just saying Mama's name.

My lips made a silent sound, more hushed than a whisper.

Mama . . . Mama . . . Mama.

I hugged myself and rocked and rocked, like Mama would if she knew demons had flung up in my dreams again.

Soon I felt morning sleep coming. Easy sleep that would let me rest a bit before I had to wake for good. As long as I kept up with my quiet call, I knew I'd feel safe.

Mama . . . Mama . . . Mama.

Near a month had passed since Parnell had taken ill. Near a month of changes and turmoil among all of us who call the Parnell plantation our home.

Most everyone at Parnell's had gone grim. For years, we'd been livin' under the same rules. Wake when the master said *wake*, work when the master said *work*, sleep when the master said *sleep*.

Now we didn't have no rules. You'd 'a thought Parnell's sickness would've been the go-'head for slacking. For the crop slaves to let the fields go fallow, and for us house servants to loaf. But each and every Parnell slave worked just as hard as ever. It was all we knew.

If I'd come to Parnell's plantation for the very first time, I'd have sworn it was Missy Claire who was suffering from some sickness, not her husband. Missy looked more wilted than a thirsty lily. While Parnell was holed up in his study, refusing to come out, Missy

Claire spent most of her time perched near the parlor window. She poked nervously at a needlepoint sampler, making little progress on it. She had dipped into a frightful silence. Her squawkiness was all but gone.

It wasn't Rance, the overseer, who was running things. It seemed Missy Claire had given all the authority over to Mama.

Mama was always the one with the strong backbone and the ability for managing folks, and now she was ruling the roost. Ruling it with hands of iron.

Mama had become downright surly. Even little things riled her. She snapped a lot. It could have been that Mama felt the burden of Master Gideon's feebleness, and the heavy duty of having to keep the Parnell homestead going.

For every annoying bit of nitpickiness that had left Missy Claire, Mama now had it double:

"Rosco, child, mind me when I speak."

"Rosco, don't drag them feet o' yours."

"Rosco, make your fetchin' snappy."

I just did like Mama said, and stayed out of her way. Soon after Parnell's stroke, Missy Claire gave in to Mama's know-how for healing. For the first time ever, she let her use the cayenne liniment to help quiet Lowell's cough.

"Kit," she'd said timidly, "maybe we ought to give your ointment a try. Now that October's come, we shouldn't take any chances with Lowell's well-being."

Then, fanning herself with one of her hankies, Missy said, "We certainly wouldn't want Lowell to catch himself any kind of cold."

Missy went on about how autumn always ushers in the threat of winter, and how Lowell was winter's sure target. (Missy Claire always thought she was an expert in the ways of weather.)

So I stirred the cayenne liniment, while Mama massaged it into Lowell's chest and back.

Oh, does that oil ever stink! It stinks worse than horse wind. But Lowell didn't seem to notice the smell. He stood obediently when Mama worked on him. He was bare from the waist up, his spindly arms held out at each side. For a moment, Lowell looked like the sack-doll I'd made for Summer. Arms stiff, body still, face blank. Even his cowlick stood at attention.

All that day I was stuck with the odor of the cayenne liniment. It had a way of clinging to my hands no matter how hard I washed them.

Mama was the one who'd been tending to Master Gideon, too. (Thea said Gideon preferred the sure-handedness of Mama's tending over Missy Claire's frail company.)

Mama served Parnell's meals to him in his study. And, with Missy Claire's go-'head, she prepared warm herb poultices, smelly concoctions Thea swore would restore the master's limp left arm and leg. (Two Sundays past, when Doc Bates came to check on Parnell, he told

Mama and Thea that even though Missy Claire gave her permission to use the poultices, they were not proven medical practice. After he left, Thea told Mama that the Lord's good herbs didn't need no practice.)

Last week, I heard Mama saying to Summer, "What I tell you—ever since Gideon's heart-shock, all kinds of official folks been comin' to this house. I spend half my day answering the door clapper."

Mama was right about that. Aside from Doc Bates, Parnell had had visits from Robert Stearns, who owns the mercantile in town, from Andrew Wells, who calls prices at the slave auctions on the block, and, just yesterday, some white-haired man I ain't never seen the likes of showed up to see Master Gideon.

"Parnell owes the man money. He's stacked himself some hefty debts, and that man wanted to make sure Parnell was still alive and able to continue with his payments," Thea had said.

To keep Master Gideon presentable for visitors, Mama arranged for Clem to bathe the master and shave his face and neck every day.

Summer still worked 'longside Mama. But something had come between them two. Some kind of heavy silence. And Summer, she was holding fast to Walnut seemed like all the time. She hugged that doll to her like it was a real, living baby.

I'd taken to giving Summer her lessons in the early blue-black mornings, after Mama had left the quarters, long before there was even a trace of sun. This was Summer's idea.

Summer now took her lessons without the lesson book I'd given her. She said Mama took the book away, for good! So, come lately, I'd been teaching Summer letters with a smooth patch of dirt and a sharp stick. I drew letters in the dirt while Summer held the lantern.

Not having a proper reading book hadn't hurt Summer any. In just two weeks she'd learned the whole alphabet. And, my addle-brained sister was more determined than ever to pay me her full attention when I insisted that we go slow with our lessons.

Ever since sickliness had taken over the master, Lowell had changed, too. His wheeziness was near to gone. If I was a firm believer in Thea's powers, I'd 'a sworn she'd put some kind of spell on Lowell—some kind of get-well spell.

He was still skinny as a whittled stick, but a flush of color had come to his cheeks. His speaking voice was still one peg up from a whisper, but he now stuttered only a little. I couldn't help but wonder if it was Mama's cayenne liniment that had done the trick, or if Lowell was somehow blessed with healing from knowing that his pa, who thought the worst of him, was sick.

Lowell and Miss McCracken were still studying "The Snow-Storm." Miss McCracken now called that part of their lesson "oratorical expression."

Lowell's "trumpets of the sky" never sounded so

good. And today, with autumn's chill starting to nip at the air, I kept those trumpets close while me and Clem worked in the toolshed.

We were supposed to be outside busting firewood to prepare for what Missy Claire had said was gonna be one of the worst cold-weather seasons Hobbs Hollow had ever seen. But clouds had painted the sky gray as flint, and, oh, were them clouds ever pouring. Outside the shed the rain slashed down in an icy, biting sheet. Missy had told us this was October's way of announcing a foul winter.

So Clem and me, we took to sharpening master Gideon's axes so's that when the rain cleared and the wood dried, we could bust and cord them logs the way Mama insists Missy Claire likes them—"twig size."

I lifted each ax off its hook and set it next to Clem, who was sharpening the blade of Parnell's biggest ax. Clem worked without speaking, his brows bent, his expression focused. He didn't even let his eyes wander when the sky threw down a whopping bolt of thunder. When Clem finished one ax blade, he extended his hand to let me know he was ready for the next.

We worked in silence through three blades. Then Clem said, "You know the hearsay?"

I shrugged. "'Bout the master holed up in his study?"

Clem shook his head.

"'Bout the visitors that been swarming round here? That the hearsay you mean, Clem?"

No again.

Clem wiped his forehead with the back of his wrist. Even in the chilly shed, he had worked up a sweat. "Naw," he said. "All that's *old* hearsay. I mean the hearsay that came to the quarters early this morning."

I'd been with Summer that morning. Our lesson had gone overtime because Summer had insisted we keep on. Clem could see by the expression on my face that I didn't have a clue.

"Missy Claire has sent for her brother, Thomas Farnsworth, who owns a plantation down in Louisiana, to come oversee things here. He'll be comin' sometime round Christmas."

There was still a question on my face. To me, this wasn't no juicy hearsay; it was just information. "So" was all I said.

Clem shook his head. "Louisiana's cotton country, Ros—the *deep* Southland, the place they sent my Marietta." Clem's words were heavy. This time he flinched when a bang of thunder escaped from the sky. "The meanest slave masters walking this earth come from Louisiana," he said quietly. "Talk at the quarters says the Missy's brother makes Lucifer look like a lamb. That he's Secesh to the core."

Another thunderclap. Clem's face went hard. His eyes darted. "I've had enough hell living here under Gideon Parnell's thumb, and it's even worse now that your mama's got me washin' and shavin' him." Clem was talking like he'd come to a decision. He said, "I didn't think so at first, but now, far as I can see, Parnell's falling sick is good luck. I'm going North to enlist in the Union army."

I shrugged, letting Clem's conviction settle for a moment. Clem waited for me to say something. More thunder came. It was a slow, rolling bellow this time.

Clem extended his hand, ready for the next ax blade. With his waiting palm stretched out full, he asked, "You comin' with me?"

If Clem had asked me about enlisting way back, when I'd first read about the Union taking in colored soldiers, I would have jumped fast as a jackrabbit.

But something in me was holding that jackrabbit back. With all that had come to pass—Parnell's heart-shock, the promise of Lincoln's proclamation, Mama taking plantation matters into her own hands— I wasn't so quick to jump.

Clem could see I was slow to answer him. He didn't badger me, but there was an impatient look coming to his eyes. All he said was, "Hand me a new blade, will you?"

13

Summer

November 10, 1862

I'D HAVE GIVEN JUST ABOUT anything, even Walnut, to have my book back. But when Mama put her foot down, she meant it, and there was no use in trying to cross her. Thanks to Rosco's teaching, I knew me all the alphabet. Plus, I knew six whole words. I came to know every bit of this without my *Clarkston Reader*.

I learned letters by finding letter look-alikes, regular things that look just like the letters in my book.

The slants of morning sunlight coming into the quarters—them light slants looked just like the letter *W*.

The wisp of hair that fell on the back of Missy Claire's neck—that was an *S*.

The trunk of the cypress tree, standing tall and proud so's even the strongest wind or the harshest words couldn't bend it—for certain, that was the letter *I*.

And them sweet, buttery peaks that formed in Mama's mixing bowl when she was whippin' tea cake batter—they were a whole mess of *M*'s, one coming up in the bowl after the other.

I'd been stringing letters together, side by side, like the pearls Missy Claire wore round her neck for the Hobbs Hollow Christmas cotillion. I'd been making my own necklace. A necklace of *P*'s and *D*'s and *U*'s and *Q*'s. Now, letters were more than curls on paper. Letters *meant* something.

I'd learned four words from Rosco: *run, man, be*, and, the longest and best word, my name, *Summer*.

Then, by accident, I learned another word by myself. Two Mondays ago, I was in the parlor where Missy Claire had been spending her days. Missy was working on her embroidery sampler, stretched in its hoop, for what seemed like the longest time. I was sitting cross-legged at Missy's feet, untangling her embroidery threads, using all the patience I could summon to stay with a tricky knot of the prettiest blue thread I've ever seen.

My eyes were starting to sting from the concentration. I took a long, slow blink, then let my gaze rest on Missy's sampler. There, plain as the day's sky, was my name, *Summer*, stitched in pink across the sampler's top arc. Further down, under the *Summer*, was a longer word. I knew all its letters. I made myself curl the sounds of them letters round my tongue. After three tries of sounding the word silently, I blurted it out. Thankfully, my blurt was quiet, like a whisper— "*Flower.*"

Missy Claire shifted her eyes in my direction. "You say something, Summer?"

I blinked and quickly turned my attention back to my knot of thread. "No, ma'am, just a breeze blowin', I guess," was my answer.

Missy Claire gave a blank smile and kept on with her needlepoint.

Already, I was starting to see what Thea meant about reading being both a blessing and a bugaboo. I was truly thankful that I was starting to see words. Sometimes I thought it was better than seeing the early morning sun crack open the shell of darkness that blanketed the sky each night. But seeing words was also like spending a whole night awake, staring into blackness. The longer I stared, the more I *didn't* see—the more words I learned, the more I came to see there were so many I just didn't know.

Missy Claire was writing carefully with her embroidery needle, crafting the letters of my name, like it was a fine, delicate thing. But what did my name have to do with flowers?

Come the next morning, I was a bushel of talk at my lesson. "Ros, Missy Claire's got my name stitched into her sampler."

Rosco was still sleepy. He wasn't fully listening.

"Missy ain't really makin' nothing with her needle and thread, Summer. Except for a few lame buds and swirls, her sampler's been bare for weeks."

I slid Walnut from my pocket and smoothed her burlap dress. "Yeah, I saw them rosebuds and swirls around the sampler's edge. But toward the center was my name. I read it, Ros. It said, *Summer*. And under my name it said, *flower*. I read that too—*flower*," I repeated.

Rosco yawned. "Missy Claire's probably makin' a sampler for the seasons. To Missy, summer ain't *you*, it's what comes after spring and before fall," Rosco insisted.

I rested Walnut in my lap, and lifted my lantern to Rosco's face. "I *know* when summer is, Ros. And I know Missy Claire don't give a toe-bone about puttin' *me* in her sampler. But summer *is* my name, and Missy's making it look special, even if summer ain't no more than a season to her."

Rosco was wincing at the lantern's light.

"I ain't never seen my name stitched into a sampler, all fine and pretty and pink. I just want to know all what Missy's sayin' about summer—and flowers," I said.

Rosco let go a heavy sigh, like he was still trying to shake off his sleepiness. "Okay, Summer," he said, "you and me, we'll go to the parlor when Missy's not there— which ain't often these days—and look for ourselves at what she's saying with her sampler."

The twilight sky was turning from black to gray. The sun's crown lit the horizon. Chief crowed. Our lesson time was almost over. "When, Ros," I said. "When we goin'?"

"Soon," Rosco said, looking off toward the fence near the toolshed, the place where Chief's call was piercing the morning's quiet.

"Folks'll be rising soon. We ain't got no more time for letters today, Summer," Rosco said.

Using the tip of Walnut's leg as my quill, I'd already written my name on the dirt strip between us. And I'd drawn a flower next to it.

Rosco picked up a sharp twig, and wrote two words after my flower: *promised land*.

I leaned in toward the dirt to get a good look. I sounded out the shorter of the two words. "*Land*."

Rosco nodded once. "*Land*," he repeated.

Then, as he did at the end of every lesson, Rosco smoothed fresh dirt over my writing and his, then tamped the dirt with his palm. And, like always, he threw down a patch of his spit to wet the dirt, and tamped again. "We best be gettin' on, Summer," he said. "A new day is coming."

14

ROSCO

November 18, 1862

I'll meet you in the mornin'
When I reach the promised land;
On the other side of Jordan,
For I's bound for the promised land.

"OLD CHARIOT," THEA'S HYMN, the one she leads off singing after evening prayers in the quarters, wouldn't leave me alone. That tired song had been grinding in my thoughts ever since Clem told me he was runnin' North. Today, when I was bringing Marlon back to the stables after a ride in Parnell's meadow, "Old Chariot" wouldn't quit haunting me. I did everything I could to push that hymn away. Even Marlon's ornery gait didn't help. Neither did the pounding of Clem's mallet shooting up from the smithing shack on the other side of the stables, where Clem was shoeing Dash.

With Parnell being sick, I now had me two horses to care for. There was Dash, Lowell's spotted mare, and Marlon, the master's own bay gelding. I'd always done the dirty work of tendin' to Marlon—mucking the stalls and such—but it was the master who worked Marlon's gait. Before Gideon got sick, he was the only one who rode Marlon. Now *I* was the only one who rode him.

I'd been tendin' horses since I was old enough to shovel hay, and I hadn't ever seen a cranky cuss of an animal like Marlon. Marlon was as stubborn as they come. And he was a big horse, sixteen hands high. There was a lot of him to put up a struggle.

I stood at the stable gate, yanking on Marlon's rein, trying to return him to his stall. "C'mon, Marlon." I clucked my tongue, but Marlon wasn't budging.

"Horse," I said, "stop actin' like a mule!"

Marlon reared his head.

"That's what I said—*mule.*"

Marlon crunched the hay under his hooves. It seemed he was thinking about his next move. This time he inclined his head toward the stall, like he was trying to show me something. Then he sputtered his horse lips, right at me.

"I been in that stall a million times, *mule,*" I said. "All that's in there is hay and the smell of horse pucky. Ain't nothin' new, so git on in." I gave Marlon's rein another tug. But Marlon stayed put.

I could feel my temper starting to flare. And to make the whole stubborn situation worse, Thea's hymn was back at me again:

When that old chariot comes,
I'm going to leave you,
I'm bound for the promised land,
Friends, I'm going to leave you.

I let up on Marlon's rein, and gave in to "Old Chariot." I sang the next verse, hoping that by letting the song spill from my lips, I could somehow set it free from my thoughts.

"I'm sorry, friends to leave you,
Farewell! Oh, farewell!
But I'll meet you in the morning,
Farewell! Oh, farewell!"

Marlon nudged my shoulder with his muzzle. He sputtered his horse lips a second time. I couldn't help but giggle. "You like my singing, huh?" (Fact is, most stubborn horses took to singing. 'Least I'd found that to be true.)

I obliged Marlon with the same verse again. Every time I sang *"Farewell! Oh, farewell!"* Marlon's hooves crept toward his stall. I let the final *"farewell"* go for several beats—*farew-e-l-l*—until Marlon had his whole front inside. There was no need to keep yanking on his rein. All I had to do was keep singing. So I did.

Slowly, Marlon made his way into his stall. But at the fifth *farew-e-l-l*, he stopped again suddenly. The *ping* of Clem's mallet was going at a steady slam. I tried to calm Marlon. "That noise ain't meant for *your* shoes," I said. "Don't let it fret you, now."

Marlon inclined his head again. I looked in the stall, thinking maybe he'd seen some kind of jumpy shadow. But it wasn't a dancing black light that halted Marlon. It was young master Lowell, peering through the stable slats from outside. All I could see of him were his eyes and brows, and the bridge of his nose. He *was* darkened in shadow, but he remained very still. It startled me all the same.

He spoke softly. Without blinking, he said, "You sing good, Rosco."

I eased backward, feeling Marlon's breath at my ear. My insides were thumping faster than moth wings near a flame. "Master Lowell?"

A kindly expression rested in Lowell's eyes. And he was looking at me in the same glad way I seen Mama look at a bud from Missy's garden that has blossomed overnight.

"Master," I said, "there's a chill out here. What brings you?"

Lowell spoke softer still. "I was looking to get some air, and I heard your singing," he said. "Can you teach me? Teach *me* to sing?" Now Lowell looked expectant.

I shrugged, then moved closer to the stable slats to match my eyes with Lowell's. Marlon must have been comforted by our closeness. His rein gave some slack, and I felt his big brown body give a little, too. He stepped fully into his stall where he belonged, right behind me. I could still feel his horse breath next to my ear.

"Singing ain't nothin' to learn," I said to Lowell. "You just do it."

Lowell said, "Not if you're cursed with a timid soul, like me."

Lowell and I watched each other for a long moment. The only sound between us was the *swish* of Marlon's tail slapping a fly that was bobbing at his hindquarters.

Finally, I spoke. I said something I've heard both Thea and Mama say many times. Now I was saying it to Lowell. "When the soul grows timid, faith will lead the way."

The late afternoon sun was beginning to bend its limbs toward the stables. A slant of light came around Lowell's face, through the slats. I squinted back the glare, which was settling on my face.

Lowell reached a hand through the slats, into the stable, and set it gently on Marlon's face. He started to sing, soft and slow.

"I'll meet you in the mornin'
When I reach the promised land . . ."

Lowell's voice was no more than a whisper. Marlon's horse lips were at it again, blowing out small sputters. After two lines of song, Lowell stopped. "That's all of the hymn I recall, Rosco," he said, stroking the white star along Marlon's nose.

I recited the rest of the first verse, my eyes never leaving Lowell's. He then sang each word with steady, gentle conviction.

> *"On the other side of Jordan,*
> *For I's bound for the promised land."*

When he was done, he said, "That's a fine song, Rosco."

"*You* the one who makes it fine, by the way you sing it," I said.

Another silence came between us. A silence different from before. It was a pleasing stillness. I was taking comfort in Lowell's company, in the natural way he was speaking to me. I couldn't help but enjoy the ease of it.

Now the sun was playing at Marlon's feet. Then Lowell came ahead with a sudden question. He lowered his voice, deliberately this time. He spoke with the understanding kindness of a brother. "You *can* read, can't you?"

I licked my lips, and groped for Marlon's rein.

Lowell said, "When the soul grows timid, faith will lead the way."

Right then, something in me let go. But I didn't let my eyes drop—I just couldn't look away. I nodded once, without answering.

More of Clem's pounding flung out from the smithing shack.

15
Summer
November 22, 1862

MAMA AND I WERE PREPARING a supper tray to take to Master Gideon in his study. My job was to set the tray with its linens and flatware while Mama made Master Gideon's supper. (She had to mash his food so's he could swallow it easy. She mashed every morsel with the exactness deserving of a baby's food.)

I was just not moving fast enough for Mama. Everything I did was wrong. When I took my care in folding the master's napkin and positioning it on the tray next to his plate, Mama came at me like a slap. She said, "I got a mind to shake you, child. Stop dawdling." Then she peered at the napkin on the tray. "The master don't like all that fancy folding. Just set the napkin by the plate."

I sucked at my teeth. "The master's got bigger problems than his napkin," I said.

Mama was standing by the window, her back to me. "Cut your sassin'," she snapped.

Since Mama wasn't lookin', I folded the napkin double.

Something in me shivered right then. An ugly thing was flaring between Mama and me. We'd had our differences, but now we were exchanging the clipped, angry words of true enemies, and it hurt.

With Mama's back still to me, I could see her shoulders tense beneath her dress. She turned to the larder, to the place where she kept the little pouch of head powders Doc Bates had prescribed for the master to stir into his tea. This was always the last item Mama put on Master Parnell's tray before taking the tray to him. The head powders were the only thing that brought the master comfort these days. Without the powders, the master's supper tray was incomplete.

Mama looked for the powders busily, sinking fully into the distraction they offered from me. The pouch of head powders stood in plain view on the windowsill, next to a pouch of sugar for tea. Both them pouches looked like one and the same. The only thing that set them apart were their marker labels.

Mama turned away from the larder. She put her hand to her cheek, pressing her memory for where the head powders might be. I could see frustration building on her face. The larder stood open behind her.

"Look to the sill, Mama," I said simply.

Mama's eyes shot to the sill. Now her expression was clouded with a mix of relief and exasperation. Her jaw went tight. Her eyes flew from the two pouches to the master's tray, then landed square on me. "Which one's the head powders?" she asked quietly.

"The one nearest to the pie you set out for coolin'," I said.

Mama lowered her eyes. She put the medicine pouch on Master Gideon's tray, then lifted the tray in front of her. "Well, then," she said, "I best be gettin' to the study."

16

ROSCO

November 25, 1862

CLEM WAS NEARLY INVISIBLE. Even with his skin as black as it was, I could barely see the likes of him. The morning was thick with a fog like I ain't never seen before. A fog that spread its gray-white cape over every inch of Parnell land. Clem sat at one end of a fallen tree trunk. I took my comfort at the tree's other end, a hollow filled with leaves. I could make out the contours of Clem's shoulders, back, knees, and hands, but the rest of him was steeped in the haze.

This was my favorite kind of Sunday morning, the kind that asks little of you. We'd seen the Parnells off to church and could now enjoy a bit of what we Parnell slaves had come to call "wearing the day like a comfortable set of clothes." (Even in his condition, Gideon attended church services. Missy

Claire believed that if he accompanied her and Lowell to "the Lord's rightful house," it would help heal him.)

Clem took in a weighty breath. "Come Christmas, I'm gone," he said. His words were soft and far away. He wasn't talking to me. It seemed he was speaking his thoughts.

He snapped a twig from his side of the tree trunk and began to tap out a random beat. The sound came slowly, a flat, lifeless clap. "The night sky's clearest in winter," Clem said. He was still talking to the fog. "When the sky's free of clouds, there ain't no trouble findin' the Diamond Eye."

I wondered if I was as ghostlike to Clem as he was to me. "What's the Diamond Eye?" I asked.

"That's what my Marietta used to call the North Star, the star that points the way to freedom." Clem went back to stilted beats with his stick.

"How you supposing to *get* gone, Clem?" I wanted to know. "You gonna run off, same way you did with Marietta?" I asked cautiously.

Now Clem was beating the tree trunk with careful, rhythmic precision. He let loose with the rattly sound of wood slapping wood. He jerked his head to the beat of his own music. "Gettin' North on foot ain't the best way," he said. "This time, I'm hitch-ridin' to freedom. Gonna let some kindly white folks take me for a ride."

I slid closer to Clem. My own head was getting caught up in the tempo of his sticks. I started to nod with the beat, which was strong and steady now.

Clem rolled out a plan. A plan that was as solid as his tree-drum. "Not every white man is pushing along with the wheels of slavery," he said. "Some think it's downright evil, and them's the ones who have gone and set up a way of helping the likes of us go North. If you and me want to enlist in the Union army, we got to get to Baltimore, then to Philadelphia, then to Boston—on rides in the white man's wagon."

"You talking 'bout the freedom trail, ain't you?" I asked. "I been hearing about them night rides in the backs of wagons, ducking and hiding in ditches and hovels all with the help of them whites folks who been calling themselves abolitionists."

Clem stopped with his sticks. He struggled to repeat my word.

"*Ab—abol—abolitionist*," he said finally. "Right, them's the ones I'm talking about."

We sat quiet for a moment. The fog began to lift its cape. "Remember what I said about Lincoln's Emancipation Proclamation that night in the quarters, the night Parnell had his stroke?" I asked.

This was one of those questions that gave Clem pause. He scratched his stick against the tree trunk's bark. He didn't answer me right off. Then he said,

"Yeah, I remember. And since that night when you spoke on it, I've caught talk of it in town."

"*What* talk?" I asked.

"Some talk," was all Clem said.

I told Clem all I knew about Abraham Lincoln's draft of the Emancipation Proclamation, how it had been presented to Congress, and how the president was planning on issuing the final and true document at the first of the new year. "If it passes, we'll be free," I explained.

"*If*. That's what they been sayin' in town about this proc—proc—proclamation, that it's all a big ol' *if*." Clem shrugged. "I can't be sittin' around waiting for an *if* to happen," he said, shaking his head. "When me and Marietta were plannin' to jump the broom, I spent night after night thinking on how fine life would feel *if* we could be together. And what a glad day it would be *if* we could get us our own place near the quarters, and start us a family.

"And I kept telling myself that maybe, just maybe, I could find a little piece of happiness livin' here on Parnell's plantation—*if* Parnell bought Marietta so's we could get hitched." Clem shook his head. "My *if*'s were all about hope back then," he said softly.

I nodded, remembering how giddy-in-love Clem had been with Marietta.

"Now," Clem said, "all's I think about is what *if*

Marietta's hurtin' somehow, wondering why I ain't come to find her. What *if* she's gone and fell in love with somebody else? And what *if* cotton country has worked her to weariness?"

Clem looked off toward the far meadow. "*If* ain't nothing but a bushel of disappointments," he said. Then he snapped his drumming twig in two and flung it to the woods.

"Freedom's ours for the takin', but we gotta take it soon, before Missy's South-lovin' brother gets here." Clem's words were clenched with determination. "You comin' with me, or you staying back to wait for Mr. Lincoln to make up his mind?" he asked.

Even with all my itching to enlist, I still wasn't so eager to follow Clem. I had a small faith in our president's proclamation, but I couldn't share my hope with Clem. He'd lost all faith in any kind of good. "I need to think things through, Clem," I said.

"What's there to think on? You want to fight for freedom or not?"

Clem was pressing at me hard. I could feel myself growing fidgety. "What kindly white men live around here who are gonna help nigras get free?" I asked. "This land's full of Secesh. Probably ain't even a single abolitionist within a hundred miles," I challenged.

"I know me one man who's on our side, and that's all I need to get gone," Clem said.

I wondered if Clem was talking truths or just fronting, trying to sound like he knew it all. "Who is it, then?" I wanted to know.

"It's the master's own medicine man, Doc Bates, that's who."

17
Summer
November 30, 1862

ON SUNDAYS, THEA LEAD A sunset worship service for us at the meeting quarters. She began this evening's service asking us to each bow our heads, and to make an appeal to the Almighty. Tonight she spoke with true conviction. "Someone among us is suffering with the pain of a long-held secret," she said. "If each and every one of us prays rightly, that soul's hurt will be healed by the Almighty's powerful hand."

Thea sure couldn't have been talking about me. The only secret I had was learning letters, and that wasn't even a secret, really. Thea, Mama, and Rosco know all about my letter learning. I had me a lot of hurt that needed healing, though. The strain that had come between me and Mama was fixing itself all the way to my bones.

I lowered my head. My prayer was simple and short. "Almighty, help me see Mama's side of things, and help Mama see into my heart just a little bit, too," I whispered.

When I finished, everyone else was still praying.

Rosco prayed with his chin rested on two fists.

Clem's eyes were squeezed shut with concentration.

Mama had bowed her head the lowest of all, and tucked it toward her chest. A tiny frown knotted her forehead. She was praying hard.

Was Mama's prayer the same as mine, that she and I would find us a patch of common ground? I wondered.

When service was over, Mama left quickly and spoke to no one at all. She went right to her prayer bench, which stood at the far corner of our sleeping quarters, facing a small window. The bench was tucked back in an alcove that was closed off with burlap draping. It was like Mama's very own little room, her private place. Her Sabbath place, she called it. The place where she said she "takes her solitude."

You could always find Mama on her bench after Sunday service. Sunday evenings were the only times she spent there. "The Lord, he's given me a slice of time on his seventh day, and for that I'm thankful," she said.

That night, as I lay on my pallet, staring hard into

the darkness, a sure and sudden ache filled me. And a shiver rose through my insides. Even with the small fire that burned in the central pit of our quarters, the nights had grown so cold. Winter was just a short time off, and the thought of winter's wind-licks—the mean slapping wind that whips its tail into the quarters at night—filled me with a heavy dread. I knew as certain as I knew my own name that the return of Mama's kindness toward me was what I needed to send my shivers away, and to endure the harsh nights of winter.

I curled Walnut into both my arms and held her as close as I could. Her little body was a welcome comfort. I slid my clenched fingers under Walnut's muslin petticoat, hoping to find a snatch of warmth. (Mama wouldn't let me take Walnut to Sunday service, so I'd been missing her this night.)

I stroked Walnut's bald, nubby head as if she had the silken hair of one of Missy Claire's china dolls. "Walnut," I whispered, "something's changin' here at Parnell's. And somethin' new is coming, too. I don't know *what's* changing or *what's* new, but *something* is. I can feel it. Same way I can feel winter pokin' its icy fingers around the corner."

Whenever I whispered to Walnut, I did it right at the place where Walnut's ear would have been—if she'd had ears—just like Rosco had shown me how to do. I was beginning to think Walnut had grown some tiny ears. She'd been listening to me for weeks now, and I truly believed that somehow she was hearing my every word. Sometimes I didn't even whisper. I just moved my lips like I was speaking, letting Walnut feel the pattern of my words forming on my lips. This worked best at night, when Mama was sleeping near me, and the quarters were as quiet as a tomb. Tonight the fire's crackle made it okay to whisper without being heard.

I told Walnut, "Oh, how I miss the way Mama used to wrap me in one of her hugs, and thank the Almighty for me, the way she'd done on my birthday."

A tiny snore rose from Mama's pallet. It was deep-sleep breathing, which hardly ever came from Mama.

Sometimes, when I spoke to Walnut, I gave a moment's pause and let myself wonder what she'd say to me if she could speak. Tonight was no different. I settled for a moment, thinking on what answers Walnut would share with me if she had a mouth and a voice for speaking. I could feel my hands growing warm beneath Walnut's petticoat. "Walnut, you're a sweet baby-doll friend," I whispered.

Soon my hands were fully warmed. I still had that ache, though. An ache that had turned to a stone in my belly. An ache that now rested in the place where the goodness of Mama's tea cakes settled after I'd enjoyed eating them.

I soon fell asleep, dreaming of sweets and walnuts and Mama and me.

When I woke, Mama had left the quarters. I hadn't heard her rustling in the dark. I'd missed the dim light of her lantern.

When Rosco and I met near the cypress tree, I told him I wanted to take today's lesson in Missy Claire's parlor. Rosco looked at me sideways. He swung his lantern in my direction. The lantern wick started to sputter, flickering its light onto my face. "You gone dim-witted, girl?" Rosco asked.

I held Walnut close. Her dress was still keeping my hands warm. "My wit ain't nowhere near dim, Ros, that's why I'm askin'. *You're* the one who said we could go to the parlor to see Missy Claire's sampler. This is the only time of day Missy ain't parked at the parlor window, stitching."

Rosco's breath rose in little puffs that billowed up in the cold air. When he spoke, the puffs shot from his mouth in spurts of white. "All right, Summer," he said, "we'll go to the parlor, but only to look at the sampler. Things ain't as risky with Parnell being sick and Missy growing so timid. But it still ain't a good idea to be having a whole reading lesson anywhere near the house."

I nodded.

Rosco set out a better plan. "We'll gather wood from

over near the toolshed first, then take it to the parlor and make like we're doing the Missy a good deed by starting a fire in the parlor for her."

"Missy's morning fire is Clem's doing," I said.

"I know," Rosco said. "But Clem builds her fire after he bathes Parnell. He sets the flame while Missy's taking her final cup of breakfast tea. Believe me, Summer, I'm sure Clem won't mind us leaving him with one less chore to do."

Without another word, I was on my way to the woodpile, with Rosco following after me.

When we got the parlor, it was black and cold and silent. Rosco crisscrossed the logs and lit them. He watched the fire logs catch, then knelt at the hearth to blow at the small flame. Slowly, the fire grew, bringing its amber light to the room.

I'd been standing at Missy's sampler hoop, holding the lantern up to its letters.

"*Summer . . . flowers . . .* " I read the words slowly and with true pleasure. Missy Claire had marked a new word onto the muslin, a word she had yet to stitch. I moved closer to the sampler to get a better look. I waved Rosco to me. "Ros, what's this say?"

Rosco kept his eyes on the fire. "*You* tell *me* what it says."

"But this here's a long word, Ros—a whole mess of letters!"

Rosco glanced up briefly. "They don't look that

messy to me. Start with the first letter and go from there."

I began with the two words I already knew, then went on to the new word. "*Summer . . . flowers . . . blo—blos—blossom— . . .*"

The fire was burning fully now. Rosco was still kneeling at the hearth to tend the fire's rising flame. "You're almost there, Summer, but there's more to the word. Stay to it," he encouraged me.

The black twilight sky was beginning to go light. Chief would be crowing soon, and our lesson would be over.

I kept with my new word. "*Blo—blossom—bl—blos—blossoming!*" The word came to me in a burst, with the same sudden beauty of a fresh new blossom. I knew there'd be more words for Missy to stitch to make the sampler a complete verse. But these few words were enough beauty to fill me up for the day.

I read all the sampler's words again and again, as if they were a fine declaration: "*Summer . . . flowers . . . blossoming . . . summer . . . flowers . . . blossoming. . . summer . . . flowers . . .*"

When I turned my gaze away from the sampler to recite without even looking at the letters, there stood Mama, her solid frame filling the doorway. She wore a strange, tight expression. "What in heaven's name are you doing?" she demanded. She was staring straight-on at me.

I felt myself flinch. Rosco stood up sharply. "Now,

Mama, don't go getting all out of sorts." Rosco was working to calm Mama by talking slow and easy. He tried to explain. "Summer and me, we thought it would be a kindly favor to get a fire going in Missy's parlor before the day even begins."

Mama was shaking her head. She still had her gaze fixed to mine, but now she'd narrowed her eyes. "You telling me a lie," she said. Her breath was heaving and angry in her chest.

"Rosco *ain't* lying, Mama," I said. "I'm the one who made him fix a fire. It was *my* idea."

Mama stood real still for what seemed like a long time. Then, in three long, quick steps, she came to where I was standing at the sampler. She didn't speak a single word. She was as close as my own shadow. She was staring hard into me. Then she said, "Takin' that book from you ain't made a bit of difference, has it? You're a thickheaded child—pig-skulled, that's what you are. Gots to learn the hard way." There was heat in Mama's eyes. It was rage.

"*Mama,*" Rosco said, still trying to calm the squall that was building fast.

"Hush up, Rosco. I know both you kids been dabbling in letters, but Summer still ain't got the sense to keep it *quiet.*"

Mama turned her sights on me—on me and Walnut. In one sudden snatch, she tore Walnut from my hold, turned on both feet, and went for the fire.

"No, Mama, *no!*" I wailed.

But it was too late. Walnut flared up in a sudden flame. All that was left of her was her head, which went black right away.

Outside, Chief's crow told us morning had come.

18
ROSCO
November 30, 1862

WHEN A TREE DON'T BEND with a storm, it snaps. That's what happened to Mama this morning. She'd surely known about me teaching myself letters, but, like she said, I didn't ever risk waving it around the way Summer did. Seeing Summer explore words openly was just too strong a wind for Mama, and something in her buckled and broke. That's why Mama punished Summer so.

It was a soul-sorry shame watching Summer's dolly burn. Later, after Mama and Summer went off to prepare Parnell's breakfast tray, it was hard to keep my mind on much else. Even when Miss McCracken came for Lowell's lesson, I was thinking about Summer and Mama and Walnut.

Miss McCracken was late. When I answered the door clapper to let her in, she was panting lightly. Her bonnet surrounded her face like petals surround the face of a flower. She was bundled in a woolen shawl. Her cheeks were flushed with the pink that cold days bring to the skin of white folks.

Lowell must have heard the clapper, too. He came to the door right behind me and greeted Miss McCracken, who unwrapped her shawl hurriedly. "Pardon my tardiness," she said. "My father's coach has been in need of repair. Doc Bates had promised to bring me today, but the good doctor never came to pick me up. I fretted for a time, fearing he'd forgotten me, then I started out walking here on my own. Walked at a good clip, I did."

Miss McCracken secured a hefty brown book under her delicate arm. She held the book firmly at her elbow, lifted her cupped hands, and blew gently to warm her palms. Suddenly remembering that she still wore her bonnet, she swept the bonnet quickly from her head. Like always, Miss McCracken's hair was twisted neatly at her nape. But her bonnet had messed the hair near her face, which now fell in wisps the color of honey.

Lowell and me, we stood side by side, listening politely to Miss McCracken. She spoke with a hefty dose of apology. This was the first time she'd ever been late for a lesson. Seemed she needed to spill the details of her delay.

She tidied her hair as she spoke. "I soon passed the Bates plantation, and thought it only proper to make certain the doctor himself had not fallen ill," she explained. "But Doc Bates was not at home. His wife, Miss Penelope, told me the doctor had been out since deep in the night hours making rounds to see patients who were sorely ailing, and that he had not yet returned. She said he'd recently made these late-night rounds part of his practice."

Miss McCracken draped her shawl over one arm. It covered the book she was holding. There was more to her story. "Miss Penelope suspects the doctor is assisting with the delivery of Jacqueline Greely's baby, over in Rudville."

Miss McCracken was fully warmed now. I could see it in the ivory that had come back to her cheeks. She placed her free hand over her heart as she continued. She wasn't looking at Lowell or me. "He's a dear man, that doctor," she said softly. "When my time comes to bear a child, I'll take comfort in knowing Doc Bates will gladly make a visit in the darkest night hour."

Then, suddenly, Miss McCracken came back to herself. She unwrapped her book from the shawl that covered it. "Well, enough time has been wasted," she said. "Let us begin our lesson."

Lowell took his teacher's shawl and bonnet and handed them to me. The shawl gave off the gentle scent that was Rose McCracken. It was the smell of woolen fibers, with a dash of barley soap thrown in. I never knew white folks had it in them—a fine scent, I mean.

I folded the shawl and carefully placed it in the front hall closet.

Right away, I made myself like a quiet, out-of-sight bird. I set my attention to the cobwebs that draped from the baluster. (Mama had been on me for nearly a week about cleaning out those cobwebs. I was saving them for today, for Lowell's lesson.)

Miss McCracken turned open her book right there in the front hall. "We'll start with oratory," she told Lowell. "And since you've made such fine and prodigious progress, we'll take your lesson to your pa's study and recite for him there. It will make him most proud, I'm sure." Miss McCracken wasn't asking a question. She was giving Lowell her lesson plan for the day.

But Lowell, he wasn't having it. A dry little cough flew out from him, followed by two hard sniffs. "Ma'am?" was all he said.

"We'll give your pa one of our favorites, Emerson's 'The Snow-Storm.'" Miss McCracken stepped past Lowell, toward Parnell's study. "Come now." She gestured with her head. "We mustn't waste any more time."

I twisted my dust rag around my finger and poked real good at the cobwebs. But I couldn't help but turn my eyes toward Lowell. His arms were folded tight around him, as if he were bracing himself against a cold wind. A second cough escaped from deep in Lowell's chest. "My pa's s-s-s-sickly, m-m-m-ma'am," he said.

Miss McCracken went to Lowell and gently placed

her hand on his forearm. "I know all about that, lad," she said. "But fine oratory is balm for the ailing."

Lowell lowered his head. Then he shook his head twice. "My pa doesn't regard me, ma'am. I'm shame to him," he said softly.

Miss McCracken lifted one of Lowell's hands and held it in hers.

"I know about that, too," she said. Now, if Miss Rose McCracken were holding *my* hand, I'd feel I had been blessed with the touch of an angel. But Lowell, he started wheezing as if someone had snatched the breath right out of him. I let my dust rag drop, and went to Lowell's side. I led him to the spindle-back bench that stood in the front hall. "He needs to sit," I told Miss McCracken.

"Indeed," she said obligingly, helping me settle Lowell onto the bench.

Lowell groped for his breath. He took several shallow sucks of air. Miss McCracken gathered her shawl from the front hall closet and draped it around Lowell's shoulders. "It ain't a chill he's got," I explained. "It's an attack of nerves that's calling up his sickly condition."

Still, Miss McCracken, whose eyes were filled with concern, kept fussing with the shawl. I stood up from the bench, about to call Mama, when Lowell spoke through a raspy bout of coughs. "I'll recite for my pa, Miss McCracken, if you come with me and stay close," he said weakly.

Miss McCracken's eyes met mine, then we both looked at Lowell. "Of course, Lowell, I'll be right there, nearby, the entire time," she said.

Lowell was breathing easier now, and his coughing had calmed.

I licked my lips. As soon as Lowell and Miss McCracken left the front hall, I fetched my rag and quietly followed them to the door of Parnell's study, where I stayed out of sight. Days before, I had found a new sheath of dust nestled near the lower hinges of the door to the master's study. This was as good a time as any to clean it.

It had been nearly two months since I'd seen Gideon Parnell up close. When I got to the study, the room was chillier than usual. A draft came from the large, arched window near the desk. Right away, I adjusted the drapes to ward off the chill, then went back to the dust at the master's door.

Mama had already begun to decorate Parnell's study for Christmas. She'd roped a garland and some Yule ribbon from the windows. In years past, Parnell's study didn't get no decorations. That's because every holiday, Parnell said the same thing. He believed "frills are best left to public parts of the house." But with Parnell spending all his days in the study, and Missy Claire spending all hers in the parlor, there were few "public parts" for the Parnells to share together in their own home.

A breakfast tray with a half-eaten bowl of hominy sat to the right of Parnell's armchair. Lowell was standing to the left of the chair, in full view of his pa. Miss McCracken stood right behind Lowell, just outside the circle of window light that surrounded the master and his son.

Gideon Parnell was a sight! He'd gone from a hefty feed-bag of flesh to a measly sack of bones. He sat slumped in his chair, his shoulders folded in around him, his feet toe to toe. The master's hands lay feebly in his lap. One of them, his left one, was all gooseflesh. It was a limp curl of fingers. And the master's eyes. They'd gone blank. Not a wink of expression to them. Parnell had become a spook.

He struggled to speak. "Git—out . . . Out—now," he stammered. The left corner of Parnell's lips tugged abruptly downward. And he slobbered when he spoke. "The boy . . . ain't got—ain't got no . . . business here," he managed. He was putting the cold shoulder to his son, as always.

At least the master was clean. Newly shaved clean, thanks to Clem. His hair, which before his stroke was usually mussed, lay obediently oiled and combed.

Lowell stood real still in front of his pa, letting his pa's uncivil words drift on by. Parnell refused to look at Lowell. Miss McCracken smoothed her skirt. "With all due respect, Mr. Parnell," she said, "I do believe Lowell has good reason to be here. He's come to share his lesson progress with you."

I worked like the dickens to remove the dust at the door, all the while keeping my hearing cocked to the conversation.

Miss McCracken folded her fingers in front of her. She said, "Lowell, please begin."

Now I was listening hard. There was a troubling silence. Then I heard Lowell take a breath. A full deep breath. He spoke slow and steady.

> *"Announced by all the trumpets of the sky,*
> *Arrives the snow . . ."*

Lowell stopped suddenly. I cut my eyes in his direction. He caught the sight of me. I pushed my chin at him. *Keep going.*

Lowell tugged nervously at the loose threads of Miss McCracken's shawl, which still hung from his shoulders. He started in again, finishing this time.

> *" . . . and, driving o'er the fields,*
> *Seems nowhere to alight: the whited air*
> *Hides hills and woods, the river, and the heaven,*
> *And veils the farm-house at the garden's end. . . ."*

Another silence filled the room. Parnell sat unmoved. If I hadn't known better, I'd have sworn I was looking at a man made of stone. A clean-shaven, slick-haired statue, staring into nothingness.

Lowell pulled his arms back around himself.

"That was quite fine, Lowell, quite fine," Miss McCracken said.

Shoot, if that had been my pa sitting there, giving me the dodge, I'd have left that room quick as flint. But Lowell just stood, front-and-center to his pa, like he was waiting for something.

Finally, Miss McCracken put her hands on both Lowell's shoulders. It looked to me like she was trying to lead him away. At first, it seemed maybe Lowell thought his teacher wanted her shawl back, because rather than follow Miss McCracken's lead, Lowell stayed by his pa's chair.

Then he did something that made me blink. He peeled off Miss McCracken's shawl, draped it around his pa, and backed away.

As Lowell and Miss McCracken were leaving the study, I saw a tiny smile on Lowell's lips, something I ain't never seen come from that boy. It was a smile of self-satisfaction.

19

Summer

December 8, 1862

THE SIGHT OF WALNUT FLARING up in a quick, hot spark had been haunting me fierce. My sweet little Walnut. My baby-doll friend. Gone. Gone to ash.

Outside, it was snowing, steady white. But all I saw was fire. The fire that ripped at Walnut's dress and arms. The fire in Mama's eyes.

I felt fire, too. A fire that had been burning in me from that cold, gray morning to this pale snowy day.

Thea and I were beating the small, braided rug that sat at the foot of the grand bed in the guest quarters. With the snow falling like it was, we were stuck to beating the rug in the storeroom, a cramped room at the side of the house where the Parnells stored brooms and buckets, washrags and wipplesticks.

"How come we're back to doing rugs?" I wanted to

know. "Missy's society meetings are long over. And besides, this ain't even a parlor rug."

Thea nodded. "Tuesday last, Missy Claire got a letter from her brother, Thomas Farnsworth, down in Louisiana. He'll be here soon to see how things is getting on since the master was struck with the heart-shock. He's gonna help manage Parnell's place for a spell."

I picked at the straw in my wipplestick.

"Come to think of it, Missy's embroidering a wedding pillow for the sister of Thomas Farnsworth's wife, who's set to marry, come June. You know how them cotton-country Southern folk is. They got a love for summer weddings. Every itty-bitty thing has got to be perfect. And they start puttin' it all together way soon ahead. Missy wants to show the pillow sham pattern to her brother when he comes, wants to get his opinion before she does any more stitching."

Thea adjusted the rug. She didn't bother looking at me when she spoke. "It's a custom in cotton country to give the bride an embroidered piece that celebrates her marrying season."

Those words from Missy's sampler danced in my memory.

Summer . . . flower . . . blossoming.

Just the thought of them pretty stitches making words put a hum up in me. "I seen that sampler, Thea. Sure is fine," I said.

Thea picked up her wipplestick and started on the rug with three steady whacks. "Thomas Farnsworth will be here in time for the Hobbs Hollow Christmas cotillion." She sucked at her teeth. "Folks is talkin' 'bout that gewgaw party like it's the coming of Baby Jesus," she said. "This year the cotillion will be held on Christmas Eve at the home of Doc Bates. Seeing as Master Parnell ain't in no condition to be gallivanting about town, Thomas Farnsworth is gonna escort Missy Claire." Thea shook her head. "Whether Missy Claire will step out for a night of merrymakin', that remains to be seen."

A burst of wool dander had puffed out from the rug and was settling to the floor. "They may have to bring the cotillion to Missy's parlor," she said with a chuckle.

Now Thea was full into beating the rug. She went at it with a whole mess of muscle. Five full blows, one after the other. "I've never seen Missy Claire turn down a party, though," Thea said. "I know that woman sure as I know how to handle this wipplestick."

I smacked the rug once at its center. "Is there anything you *don't* know, Thea?"

Thea stepped back from the rug. "No," she said.

"Then you know about Mama taking my book. And you know about my dolly."

Thea leaned her wipplestick along the doorjamb. She gazed at me with kindness in her eyes. "I do," she said gently.

That fire was still burning up in me. It lurched when I talked about Walnut.

"You got every reason to feel the heat that's rising in you, Summer. But you listen good to your Thea, now. Your dolly's in a new place, Walnut is. She's in *Serendipity*."

I set my wipplestick next to Thea's. This was the first time we beat a rug together that Thea let me slack. "Where's Serendipity?"

"That's the place all the broken-headed china dolls and the stuffing's-all-gone rag babies go when they ain't no more use to the children that owns them."

Like always, I had to let Thea's words settle for a moment.

"What about dolls that been burned up by their young'uns' mamas?"

"Serendipity's for them too. And, oh, believe me, child, when I tell you that Serendipity is *beautiful*." Thea's eyes got wide. She looked toward heaven when she spoke. "In Serendipity there ain't no pain. There ain't no masters. And there sure ain't no fires. And all them china-headed dolls and rag babies play real good together. Ain't no fighting or hatred in Serendipity, neither."

I lifted my wipplestick. I slapped it to the rug a second time. "This sounds like what you sing about at services, Thea. Sounds like the promised land."

"Call it whatever you want. All's I know is,

Walnut's there right now, eatin' tea cakes with some china-faced sweetheart who's praising her for how smart she is."

Sometimes I think being a seer has messed with Thea's head. Lots of days, she's full of crazy seer-talk. Made-up stories and strange ways of putting things. This was one of those days, and I didn't have the wherewithal to put up with such foolishness. I couldn't tell if Serendipity was real, or just a bunch of hogwash. Walnut was cinders now. That I knew for true.

I paid no more mind to Thea's Serendipity. I had more important things prodding at me. "My mama hates me, don't she," I blurted.

"Your mama hates what she can't have. The power you've taken in finding letters is just one piece of what she can't have. But your mama's wanting in other ways, too," Thea said.

Thea was fraying my nerves. I couldn't help but tell her about herself. "You're always spinning double-talk—talking riddles and folly. It's enough to make a person loony!"

Thea rested a hand on her hip. "There ain't no riddle to what I'm sayin', child. I only speak in truths."

"Truths only *you* can understand."

"Truths you'll come to know by speaking to your mama."

"How can I talk to Mama if Mama don't hardly talk to me, come lately?"

"In a logjam it don't matter how strong the stream's

current is. One of the logs has got to budge first, else the jam stays a jam."

I bit the underside of my lip. *Seer-talk. Riddles and folly.*

When we'd finished in the storeroom, we rolled the rug and carried it back to the guest quarters. As we passed the small window at the first landing of the main staircase, I took a hard look at the snow outside. It had spread its petticoat over every inch of Parnell land. It was a sugar-snow, white and sparkly. But I struggled to find its beauty. I still had a fire churning up inside my belly.

20
ROSCO
December 15, 1862

IT'S TIME FOR ANOTHER LOOK-SEE in the master's study. Another birthday, when Gideon Parnell calls me in and pays me some attention. Usually he does most of the talking. But this time I'm the one who's saying the most. I want something from my master, and the only way to get it is to ask.

When I appear in his doorway, Gideon says, "Don't be scared, I don't bite." He's leaning full back in his armchair, holding his spectacles in one hand.

I say, "I ain't scared." But I'm feeling afraid. Still, I let the master know what's on my mind. "I need to speak to you about something."

Gideon nods, gives me the go-'head to keep on talking.

"I'm lookin' to marry—to get hitched with the Union army," I say.

Parnell puts on his specs. Peers at me for what seems like a long time. Scratches his chin. He's thinking on something. Finally he says,

"Tell me why you want to hook up with this Union army. The Union army ain't good for boys like you. She'll fill your head with all kinds of foolery."

I start to tell Parnell that the Union is good for me, and for everybody who wants freedom. And, I'm thinking I should tell him, too, that the Union army wants me. Wants me badly. Wants me to come fight.

But before I can even get the words out, I notice a crack in the floorboard that's opening up under my feet. Out from the crack pokes the head of a strange, black snake, a kind of snake I can't name.

Soon the snake is slithering out fast. It grows longer and longer, curling and twisting its ugly black body through and around my ankles.

When the snake ties itself into a knot at my shins, I come to see this is no snake at all. It's the overseer's whip, come to life, squeezing the living wits out of me, and roping me down to the master's floor.

"The Union can't take you so soon," Master Gideon says with a little laugh. "I won't allow it."

With that snake still at my shins, somebody was prodding me to wakefulness. "Ros! Wake up!"

Had Mama come to comfort me?

"Ros! Ros!" When the voice came a second time, it wasn't Mama's.

"Wake up, Ros!"

I shuddered. Except for the glowing coals in the pit at the center of the quarters, the room was black. A heavy hand nudged me. "Clem, that you?"

"Throw your britches on, Ros! Move quick, 'else we gonna miss it!"

My mind was a jumble. It was telling me two things at once.

Hurry up! Hold back!

I scrambled for my britches. Clem came into view. His face was a shadowy form, lit blue-brown by the coals. He was poking at my shoulder. I could hear the town hall clock striking in the distance—nine . . . ten . . . eleven . . . twelve. . . .

Midnight.

"What is it, Clem? What *is* it?" I was talking as loud as a person fully awake. I heard Mama stir on her pallet.

Clem pressed two fingers to his lips. "Shhh." He tugged at my sleeve. He motioned to the door of the quarters. "Just come on," he whispered.

Without a lick of good sense, I followed Clem down the plantation entry road. The moon was out, spreading its cream over Parnell's land. I could see clear to the far fields, where haycocks stood like hunchbacked giants. It was unusually warm for a December night. We'd had a snowfall a few days back. It had covered everything but had melted the very next day. There were leftover patches of white, though, clinging to tree roots and the roof of the toolshed.

Before we were even halfway to the end of the entry road, I saw why Clem had pulled me from my pallet.

There was a night vigil winding along the lane at the edge of Parnell's property.

Clem and I made our way to the low stone wall that separates the plantation from the lane. We stayed low, crouching just enough to see over the top of the hedge. We had a clean view. A slow, quiet parade passed in front of us. There were whispers and whimpers floating out from the group. But their eyes stayed ahead. They each held a burning candle, piercing the dark with a flickering ribbon of light.

"Where they goin'?" I asked.

"To the church for a midnight service. Three Confederate soldiers from Hobbs Hollow were killed two days ago, fighting in the Battle of Fredericksburg, just south from here. Them nightwalkers are going to pray for the souls of the soldiers."

"How come they're taking to the lane so late at night?"

"To keep watch over the bodies," Clem explained. "There's been a pack of body-robbers round these parts, people stealing the dead before they're even rested in their graves, and selling 'em to the medical college in Winchester, for those that's learning to be doctors. The body-robbers strike in the deepest nighttime. When the vigil gets to the church, the townsfolk will sit till daybreak, till it's safe to leave the fallen soldiers."

Crouching behind the stone wall was putting an ache to my knees. But I stayed low, watching and listening to Clem.

"When I went to town today to get a razor strop for the master's shavin' kit, the Battle of Fredericksburg was all the talk," Clem told me. "I passed through Littleton Square, where folks was saying the fighting started when an army of Union soldiers came up along the Marye's Heights hills. They came storming, trying to attack. But the Confederates, they held 'em off. Held 'em off, and *killed* 'em off at the same time. Folks in town was saying them Northern boys was fallin' fast and hard. It was an ugly defeat for the Yanks, and a bloody one, too."

The band of townspeople seemed to grow, bringing more light to the lane. The walkers were mostly women and young'uns.

"It was the North who lost the battle," Clem said, "but it was Hobbs Hollow that lost some of its very own soldier boys."

The sky above us was a clear, wide blanket of black, dappled with stars. It looked like heaven was having its own vigil of tiny lights. "Who from Hobbs Hollow went down in the attack?" I asked.

"There was Ben Stokes, whose pa, Travis, is a good friend of the master's. There was Russell Appleton, that skinny, freckled boy who used to live over by near where Doc Bates's plantation is. And there was Johnny Kane, Miss Rose McCracken's beloved, who she was set to wed, come the harvest."

No sooner had Clem spoken Miss McCracken's

name did I spot her among the mourners. Her head was lowered toward the sputtering wick of her candle. From what little I could see, it looked as if she was weeping.

I didn't even know Rose McCracken had a beloved. She never once mentioned Johnny Kane's name. Seeing her pass in a wash of sorrow filled me with an unspeakable sadness. I sure didn't want the South to win the war. And I didn't much care that friends of the master's had lost boys in the fight. But I did care that Rose McCracken's beloved had fallen. Rose didn't deserve no kind of hurt. I watched her trudge along the lane with the rest of the grief-stricken group. Soon the sight of her was lost to me among the procession.

Clem said, "You know what this all means, don't you?"

I shrugged. To me, all it meant was that a grim night had come to some white folks in Hobbs Hollow.

"The Union army needs us, Ros. They need us now, more than ever. Fredericksburg put the South on the one-up. Next time, it could be worse for the Union. And if the Confederates get to feeling too cocky, it'll be harder for us to get North. The South'll be spreading its Secesh pride by seeing how many escaped slaves it can round up and bring back to Southern soil. If we wait too much longer, we'll end up like them dead soldiers, 'cept we'll be dead before we even have the chance to become fightin' men. And once Missy Claire's brother brings his cotton-lovin' self to Parnell's, getting North is gonna be all the harder."

The vigil had fully passed us now. Their candlelit march trailed off up the lane, closer to town. Clem and I were left alone under the light of the moon and stars.

"See that—the Diamond Eye. The North Star." Clem pointed. "It's showing us the way, Ros. The way to freedom."

I let my gaze follow Clem's finger to the brightest star in the sky. It truly *was* a diamond. A jewel nestled in a spread of black velvet.

Clem and I were silent for a long time. We each slipped into our own thoughts. The Diamond Eye watched us from above. I gave that star a long, hard look. That's when it came to me: I was truly doubtful about running North.

Doubt is one of those things that creeps up slowly for days and days, then pounces. Tonight it had me pressed under its paws. And without me saying a single word, Clem knew it. "You backsliding, aren't you, Ros—having second thoughts," he said.

I didn't even have to answer.

"Ros, *you* the one who told *me* you wanted to enlist."

"You're right, Clem. I ain't denying it. But if I flee, I'll be leaving all that I know—Summer, Mama, even Marlon, the master's horse." I didn't mention Lowell or Miss McCracken. There were pieces of each of them that I was slow to leave behind, too. "Besides," I said, "if Abraham Lincoln's proclamation passes at the first of the year, like it's supposed to, we got freedom coming soon. Real soon."

Clem sucked at his teeth. "*If,*" was all he said.

I took to speaking my piece carefully, trying to make Clem understand. "What about Parnell being so sick? Who's gonna help Mama care for him if we're gone? Who's gonna look out for Summer? And who will tend to Marlon?" Not only was I having doubts about leaving Mama and Summer, and Parnell's stubborn horse, but that snake-dream hadn't fully let go of me. I said, "You know what happened the last time you ran, Clem. Ain't you scared of the whip?"

"I'm more scared of stayin' a slave," Clem said.

Clem flung a pebble high over the top of the hedge. He said, "Seems you don't have that problem, Ros. Seems you ain't nothin' but a white man's critter."

21
Summer
December 18, 1862

I WAS SUFFERING A FIT OF sleeplessness when I heard Mama rise from her pallet. Mama bundled in a woolen blanket. She gathered her lantern and went to her prayer bench. The blanket's tail dragged behind her as she made her way.

I couldn't tell if it was night or near-morning. The quarters were quiet as a burial yard, but twilight's gray seemed to be filling our cabin. One thing was for certain: It sure wasn't Sunday. Mama was taking her slice of solitude during a time other than the Sabbath.

I followed Mama without her hearing me. When I pushed aside the burlap draping that set Mama's prayer bench apart from the rest of the quarters, Mama was hunched in her blanket. Her head was lowered toward her hands. Like always, her back was to anyone who entered the private place. I slipped around to Mama's side to watch her pray.

Mama's lantern rested next to her on the bench. Her blanket was peeled back at her lap. When I took a hard look, I saw that she wasn't praying at all. She was holding an open book! She was holding my lesson book, my *Clarkston Reader*, smoothing its pages as if they were fine silk! Her dark, gnarled hands moved carefully across the book's parchment.

I blinked. My squirreliness got the best of me. "*Mama.*"

Mama quickly pulled the blanket in around her. She turned at me with a startle. She looked shamefaced. "Summer, Summer, child," she stammered. "Daybreak's a ways off. Chief ain't crowed yet. I'm praying, is all. Go back to sleep, now."

I shook my head no, and came closer. "My book, Mama. You got my book."

Mama's body, blanket and all, let go a sigh. She was dumbstruck. I slid onto the bench next to her.

Mama gently closed the book. Its handsome cover stared up at us. With the lantern's glow spreading across its leather, that book looked like a newly found treasure.

"You know letters, Mama?" My eyes had gone wide.

Mama shrugged. "Not a one."

"Do you want to know them?" I asked.

"No, child," she said plainly.

The very sight of my lesson book started me to remembering how much I loved learning letters from *The Clarkston Reader*. Or from anyplace, for that matter. Seeing as Mama had the book right here, I was gonna try my best to show her that reading was far from evil.

"I could teach you, Mama," I said. "We could learn letters together. Then *you'd* see what *I* see in all them curly shapes."

Mama turned to face me on the bench.

I said, "Learning letters is the same as when you make Missy's Claire's tea cakes or do her hair. Or help clear young Master Lowell's lungs during one of his wheezing fits. There's a true special beauty to doing each of them things. A gift that comes only from you. That's called *arts*, Mama—a fine and fancy way of making or doing something." I was talking as fast as I could, pushing to get my words out before Mama shushed me. "You been knowing how to make special, beautiful things since forever, Mama. You're the only one who can make them the way you do. That's 'cause you found your art. And your art makes you happy, don't it, Mama?"

Mama nodded. "It does," she said. She was giving me the courtesy of listening carefully.

"Reading is arts *and* letters. Beauty and know-how, all in one," I said.

I told Mama about my letter look-alikes. How she could even find letters in everyday things.

Mama shook her head. "Reading ain't the same as doing hair and making tea cakes. It just ain't, Summer. And I can't just learn to read, like you done. It ain't so simple as that."

"You could learn to read if you *wanted* to."

"*Don't* want to," Mama said firmly.

Mama turned her eyes to the floor. "Even if I did want to make sense of all them letters, I ain't got the muster for it."

I leaned in toward Mama. "But, Mama," I said, "how do you know you can't read if you ain't never tried it?"

Mama tugged at her blanket. "I did try it once, Summer," she said quietly. "Long, long time ago."

I glanced sidelong at Mama. "Rosco showed you?" I asked.

Mama avoided my eyes. "No," she said. "It was before Rosco and you was born."

"Who, then?" I wanted to know.

Now Mama looked at me straight. "Gideon," she said softly.

I had to make sure I was hearing right. "*Master* Gideon?"

Mama nodded. Her eyes jumped from me to the book in her lap, then back to me again. There was more coming. I could tell by the pained expression filling Mama's face.

Mama set the lesson book to one side of the bench. She held both my hands in hers. "Summer"—she was weighing her words—"Gideon Parnell, he's got a good heart."

A smirk came to my lips. "Anybody who's sick with heart-shock ain't got a good heart."

"Please, Summer, don't give me lip. Not now."

I pulled my hands from Mama's hold. I folded my arms tight in front of me.

"When I first came here to the Parnell plantation, I was a bit older than you are now. And, like you, I was getting near to my woman years. Gideon had just taken over the plantation from his pa, who'd died not long before. Gideon's the one who brought me here. Purchased me from the sale of slaves at the Thornton plantation, down in Georgia. When I left Thornton land, I left everyone I loved—my own mama and pa, two of my sisters, and my baby brother, Jacob. It was a down-low hurt to be torn from my family like that. Hurts still."

Mama had already told me how she'd come to Parnell's. I already knew the pain that slave-selling brings, and I knew about Mama's worry that me or Rosco would be sold away.

I was wanting to hear about Gideon showing Mama to read. "Telling me about being brought to Parnell's from the Thornton plantation don't have nothing to do with letters, Mama," I said, shifting on the bench.

"It's got everything to do with it, Summer, if you just let me speak." Mama squared my shoulders in her hands so's I'd listen. "When I first came here, Gideon took a liking to me right away. And I took a liking to him. He was strong and handsome. A dandy, he was."

"A dandy what?"

Mama still held me firm. She talked on, past my sassin'. "Seeing as Master Thornton had baptized me as a Christian, Gideon gave me a Bible of my very own. But I couldn't use that Bible, 'cause I didn't know how. That's when Gideon first showed me letters, and tried to teach me to read. I fell in love with the possibility of understanding all them holy words." Mama took a slow breath. "And I fell in love with Gideon Parnell," she said.

Just then a tight stab pounded at my chest. I was too stunned to speak.

But, Mama, she had plenty more to say. "It wasn't long till I was in the family way with Rosco, then later with you." My insides were turning somersaults. My legs were as heavy as Clem's horseshoe iron. I thought my hearing was playing tricks on me. But my voice came back to me right then. "Gideon Parnell is my *pa?*"

"He is," Mama said weakly.

Silence.

"How come Rosco don't know none of this?" I was still trying to make sense of it all myself. "Rosco knows everything," I reasoned.

"Rosco ain't never asked me about his pa because he knows the truth of it in his bones, without askin'."

My breathing had gone short. "Why don't you just tell Rosco, then?"

Mama didn't answer right off. "Rosco knows that if he don't ever ask, and don't ever hear me utter the truth, then he can live like it *ain't* the truth."

There it was again. That word. *Truth.* It had a way of following me around—first in Parnell's study, and now here with Mama and me. Seemed to me truth was a lantern bright enough to light the road, but harsh enough to show the grit along the way.

My innards were churning something fierce. *Gideon Parnell. My pa.*

"Does Master Gideon know he's our daddy?"

Mama nodded. "'Course he does. He just don't tell it out to people. He *can't* tell it out." Mama grew thoughtful for a moment. She said, "Gideon takes a quiet pleasure in seeing you young'uns grow. That's why he asks to see you on your birthday. It's his small, secret way of being your pa."

There was even more to what Mama had to tell me—more truth. She let me settle a bit. Then she spoke again. "When Gideon took over his pa's plantation, folks said the plantation was sure to suffer. Said Gideon didn't have the salt to run things. People laughed and laughed about the future of the Parnell legacy.

"At that same time, nigras learning letters was gathering a heavy dose of attention in these parts. Plantation owners were watching their slaves with possum eyes. Any time it came to light that a nigra knew letters, the white folks in town talked a vicious streak about whoever it was that owned that slave. Said the master couldn't keep control of his own property. And the nigra who got found out met with the bullwhip, or got sold from them that was their own family.

"With all the talk 'bout reading, and with all that folks was sayin' 'bout Gideon—putting him down and such—Gideon took a quick hatred to nigras learning to read. He took my Bible right back, too.

"The whole mess was made worse when Lowell came along, all sickly. When Lowell was born, Gideon knew that the Parnell family name would surely suffer the strikes of a bad reputation. Gideon was determined to do all that he could to prove every other plantation owner wrong. To show everybody that a Parnell man can handle his slaves, he took a hard line on letter-learning and books, as far as his nigras were concerned. Told me if I ever took to letter-dabbling, he'd have no choice but to sell me off from here." Mama let go a heavy breath.

I twisted free of Mama's hold. Her hands on my shoulders were riling me.

"You can best believe I didn't have to give none of Gideon's words no second thought. When I birthed you and Rosco, I knew I'd been given two special gifts," Mama said. "But I had to keep quiet 'bout where the gifts come from. Couldn't tell a soul 'bout who was the pa of you children. But that didn't fret me, and it still don't. I was so happy to have been blessed with my own family, all right here with me." Mama's face softened.

"I knew I'd find pleasure in learnin', but I put the notion of learnin' to read right out my head. I didn't want to have to hide another happy secret. It's hard to sweep your joy under a bushel. It hurts. As much as I wanted to learn letters, I didn't want to have to keep one more joyous thing locked up. So I turned away from reading and never looked back.

"You see, Summer, having babies don't invite no suspicion or no trouble. Letter-learnin' invites both. With you children as mine to raise, I couldn't risk diggin' into something that could bring on reasons for losing you or having me sold away."

I sat real still. Now *I* was giving *Mama* the courtesy of listening.

"I would surely love to learn to understand the teachings of the Bible, the way they're outlined in the book itself. But I just can't, Summer. I can't."

My hands had begun to tremble. I slid them between my backside and the bench.

"Anyways, I got to thinkin' 'bout that Bible Gideon once gave me. That's when I took out your lesson book. I been keeping it hid here in my prayer place, waitin' for a good time to take it back to the house without nobody seeing."

Mama brought *The Clarkston Reader* back to her lap.

"I'd be dishonest if I didn't admit to taking a certain enjoyment from lookin' at the book's cover. It's got the same heft and beauty as the Holy Book."

Mama traced the swirls along the book's top corner. Her fingers were bony as ever. They were strong fingers, though. Strong like all of Mama.

"I'm sorry 'bout snatching this here reader from you, Summer, " Mama said gently. "With Gideon's heart-shock, and with all this talk about letters, I been out my head lately. And I been fretting for the longest time 'bout the book being stolen from the master's study."

Mama looked right at me. "Sooner or later, the book's gotta go back to the plantation house, Summer. Ain't no choices in the matter."

As much as I loved *The Clarkston Reader*, I had done me plenty of letter-learnin' without it. "That book ain't no use to me now, anyways," I said.

"I'm sorry, too, 'bout Walnut," Mama said softly. "Ever since that day in Missy Claire's parlor, I been prayin' for your forgiveness."

There was wetness coming to my eyes—my hooty-owl eyes, the same green eyes as my master's. Silence had me by the tongue again. I started to cry. Strange tears were rising out from me. I was missing Walnut. My sweet little baby-doll friend, who wasn't here for me to hold.

I was crying for Mama, too. Mama, who'd had the gift of reading yanked out from under her.

Mama and I both turned to the window. Dawn's first

pale light met each of our faces. I was hoping to see the sun lifting up over the fields. But a thicket of clouds covered the sky instead.

Mama and me, we were through with words. There wasn't no more talkin' to do.

PART THREE
Old Chariot

22
ROSCO
December 20, 1862

"**N**OTHIN' BUT A *white man's critter.*"

Clem's words poked at me for days and days. Poked at me good.

Last thing I am is a critter. Dogs is critters. Coons is critters. *I* ain't no critter.

Mama had put me to work, making pine wreaths to hang on each door of the Parnell home. Thomas Farnsworth would be arriving any day now, and Missy Claire told Mama she wanted the house to look festive when her brother approached.

So here I was in the cramped side-door anteroom, near the back steps by the scullery, stitching together the limbs of a bough. Last thing I wanted to be doing was making wreaths. Them pine needles were prickly. And the fastening twine kept tangling between the branches. But today was Lowell's lesson day, and at least

I'd get to see Miss McCracken. The side-door window offered the best view of the lane, so I'd be sure to see her coming before her carriage even turned onto Parnell's entry road.

I worked as best I could to make sure the wreaths were stitched tight. As I knotted a lick of twine, a tiny winged beetle crawled from one of the pine branches. Crawled right onto my thumb and scuttled its way up my wrist, even as I stitched. I winked shut with one eye, and set the other eye to watching him go. Now *this* was a critter. "You headed someplace special?" I asked.

Soon as I spoke, that beetle stopped in its tracks. "Don't be scared now. I ain't got a mind to hurt you," I said softly. If I could've seen that beetle's little bug eyes, I would've sworn they were looking right at me. He considered me for a moment, then kept on with his beetle walk. He was determined to keep going. And he did.

I set down my work and watched that little bug take himself over the wrinkles of my shirtsleeve, all the way to my shoulder. He made a slow climb. He never stopped to rest.

I kept still as stone, with my arm held out in front of me. When the beetle reached the place where my sleeve met my shoulder, he quickly flew up. I watched him hover in the air above me, then land on the doorjamb. When I opened the door and let him out into the cold, white day, I realized that little lowly bug—that critter—had more freedom than I did.

It took me the better part of the morning to finish the wreaths. I stitched four in all, three small ones and one big one for Parnell's front door.

I set the wreaths around the anteroom floor to admire my handiwork. Mama would be pleased.

Just then, the sound of hooves came along the lane. It was Doc Bates's wagon. He was most likely bringing Miss McCracken. I watched from the window. There was no sign of Rose. A sudden clap came to the front door. I hurried to answer it. Doc Bates stood alone on the doorstep. He was holding a drawstring pouch in one hand, and what looked to be a folded *Harper's Weekly* in the other.

He said, "I'll be sure to catch the pleurisy if I stand out here in the cold. May I come in?"

I widened the space between us to let the doctor enter. "Yessir, doctor sir. Come in." A draft had come in through the open door.

Doc Bates took off his hat. "The pleurisy's rampant in these parts. I can't afford to take ill before the Christmas Eve cotillion, which will be swarming my very own parlor in just a few days." The doctor sighed. "My Penelope will skewer me for certain if I come home coughing. A sick host dampens the holiday cheer of his guests—and his wife."

I hardly ever had the chance to see Doc Bates up close. And this was the first time we'd spoken. There was something familiar and calming in the doctor's eyes. He had the same easy way about him as Miss McCracken. His lips were settled in a tiny smile of contentment. The hair on his head had been mashed by his hat.

Doc Bates was a stately man. Tall. Upright. Shoulders as square as the corners of the entry hall clock, which was now giving off two chimes. "It's young Master Lowell's lesson time," I said. "Have you brought Miss McCracken with you?"

The doctor shook his head. "It'll be long past the New Year before Rose McCracken sees fit to teaching again. That young lady is forlorn beyond mention. She's suffered the loss of her beloved, young Johnny Kane, who fell in the Battle of Fredericksburg not even a fort-night ago."

I did my best to look like I was dumb to the news of Johnny Kane. "What brings you, then?"

Doc Bates held up the drawstring pouch. "I've brought a ration of head powders for Gideon."

"I'll tell my mama you've come to check on the master," I said, stepping away toward the kitchen.

But with gentle firmness, the doctor fetched me back before I even had a chance to go. "Oblige me with a chat first, won't you?" he said.

I looked at him sidelong. "Sir?"

"I guess Gideon has neglected to teach his servants the duties of cordiality." That little smile hadn't left the doctor's lips.

"Cordiality, sir?"

The doctor came closer to me. He lowered his voice. "What's your name?"

I cut my eyes toward the master's study, wondering if Parnell could hear us having some "duties of cordiality." Then I glanced to the stairs to see if Lowell was coming for his lesson. There was no sign of him.

"Rosco," I said, near a whisper. "Rosco's my name."

"Rosco," said the doctor. "You ever watch the stars at night, Rosco?"

I didn't answer one way or the other. All I did was shrug. Doc Bates may have been an easy talker with a smile on his lips, but he was still a white man. Still an acquaintance of Parnell's. Who knew where his cordiality was heading? I couldn't help but wonder why the doctor was trying to draw me out. You can never tell with white folks.

Doc Bates set the pouch of head powders on the hall bench. He unfolded his newspaper and, with both hands, curled it into a thick, tight roll. "Well," he said, "if star-watching ever strikes you, you can use this." He swung his rolled newspaper to the ceiling and peered through one end. "Not quite a telescope, but it will bring the North Star into brilliant isolation. Especially on a clear night," he said.

Then Doc Bates did something that made me blink. He pressed the paper roll right to my chest. "I hear more and more young nigras are learning to read. If you're one of them, this may interest you. If you don't know letters, find someone who does—someone you trust."

Doc Bates was speaking near to a whisper. He said, "This . . . this star-finder is best used at night and in out-of-the-way places." Doc Bates was standing over me, looking clear into my face. I couldn't hold his gaze, though. Its openness startled me. I didn't know what-all to do. I quickly lowered my eyes.

The doctor rocked once on his heels. "I'll take the head powders to Gideon myself. No need to call on your mama. I know the way."

Before Doc Bates disappeared into the gray shadows of the master's study, he said, "Let me know if you ever need anything, Rosco. I'm a man of healing."

I dared to look at Doc Bates then. Straight and long, I looked. There was something more than openness in his eyes. There was invitation. Doc Bates was encouraging me to action. Clem had been right. What he'd said about the doctor's involvement with abolition had been true.

I went back to the anteroom by the scullery. I turned that paper open quick as I could. It wasn't the *Harper's Weekly* at all. It was called *L'Union*, a newspaper written by free coloreds in Louisiana! I didn't even know there could ever be such a thing—a whole newspaper made by nigras, written by colored men!

The paper was dated December 6, 1862. It told of Abraham Lincoln's draft of the Emancipation Proclamation. It urged coloreds to fight for freedom. It said:

> *Men of my blood! Shake off the contempt of your proud oppressors. Enough of shame and submission; the break is complete! Down with the craven behavior of bondage! Stand up under the noble flag of the Union and declare yourselves noble champions of the right. Defend your rights against the barbarous and imbecile spirit of slavery . . .*

Like a blurred carriage on the horizon that suddenly comes into view, I now knew the true purpose of Doc Bates's visit. Doc Bates was offering me his help to go North. And to think it! If I was to get free, I could read and write openly, maybe even in a newspaper.

With a firm grip, I curled the *L'Union* back to its roll. I looked through one end. I studied the ceiling coffers.

I now had the call from *L'Union* poking at me: "*Defend your rights against the barbarous and imbecile spirit of slavery . . .*"

23
Summer
December 22, 1862

"**K**IT! KIT!"

There was no mistaking Missy Claire's call. It flew out from her dressing chamber like a nilly goose flails up from her just-laid egg.

Mama and I were in the kitchen, preparing the master's breakfast tray. "Quick," Mama said, "set a tray with tea service and meet me in Missy Claire's chamber." Mama hurried to tend to Master Gideon, then to Missy Claire.

This was the day Missy Claire's brother, Thomas Farnsworth, was set to come. Mama had woken me early and had insisted I leave the quarters with her at first light, way before Chief's crow. I tried to remember what Mama had told me about Missy Claire: that I should be mindful of the hardships Missy Claire had suffered. Since this had never come easy to me, I figured I could at least make some pretty-looking tea for Missy Claire on the day she was expecting her brother. So I set a real fine tray, I did. Silver. Linens. China. Doilies. And a tea sock with Thea's best mint leaves. As I made the tray, I tried to imagine how I would feel if Rosco was coming to visit me, after not seeing him for a whole long time. Maybe that's what Mama meant by *mindfulness*—putting myself inside somebody else's circumstances.

When I got to the dressing chamber, Mama was sitting at the vanity with Missy Claire, preparing her hair for dressing. Missy Claire was leaning in toward the looking glass that hung above the vanity. "I look absolutely ghoulish!" Missy Claire was saying. She handed Mama her ivory-handled brush. "Curl quickly," she said. "My brother Thomas prides himself on his punctuality, and he's scheduled to arrive this very morning, soon after the breakfast hour."

Mama put the bristles to Missy Claire's hair. She smoothed it and parted it and curled it. When she was through, I helped Mama dress Missy Claire. First, we dressed her in brown watered silk. But Missy Claire frowned at her reflection in the looking glass. She said the color brown left her face looking pale. So we undressed her all the way down to her satin slip, fitted her with a fresh petticoat, and dressed her back up again, this time in a flounced dress of emerald green. This brought an even darker frown to Missy Claire's face. She insisted that the flounces accentuated her poorly. Mama tried to make Missy Claire come to reason. "The breakfast hour is close," she said. "Your brother's most likely near to town by now. I'm sure he'll be pleased to see you, whatever you be wearing, even if you was to greet him in a gunnysack."

Missy Claire huffed. "A gunnysack! Oh, Kit, don't taunt me with such foolery."

Finally, Missy Claire settled on a simple dress of French blue dimity. To me, the dimity made her look palest of all, and it showed off her scrawny arms and her chicken neck. If it had been me, I would have chosen the emerald green. Even a chicken looks good in flounces.

Missy Claire studied herself in the vanity looking glass. "Summer, child, help me with my pearls. I want to wear them today, in honor of my brother's arrival. The pearls belonged to our mother, Leona. The sight of them will surely please Thomas after his long journey."

I'd only *seen* Missy's pearls, had never been obliged to *touch* them. Even though Missy was telling me to help her, it seemed I needed some kind of special permission to lay my hands on her delicate jewelry. I looked to Mama.

"You heard what Missy Claire's askin'," she said, real low. "Go 'head, now—git the pearls." Mama nudged me.

I lifted the pearls from their velvet-lined box that

sat on top of Missy Claire's vanity table. They were heavier than I expected they'd be, but the weight of them was joy to me. My hands trembled as I fastened the clasp at Missy Claire's nape. Those pearls were milky dots of beauty, even on a chicken neck.

Missy Claire stood quickly. She smoothed her dress, patted her hair, and swept from the chamber. Mama looked to see that Missy Claire had fully left the room. Quietly she said, "If I ever see freedom in my lifetime, one of its greatest glories will be the power to choose—whether it's a dress, or a 'do, or a spoon to stir my tea."

Mama was speaking more to the walls than to me. But still, I nodded once firmly. "I'd choose to wear pearls," I said.

Mama followed Missy Claire in a flurry, taking the tea service with her. As she left, she told me to straighten Missy Claire's bed linens and to fluff her pillows. That pleased me fine. Mama usually fixes Missy Claire's bed—and fetches her jewelry—but today some kind of good luck was smiling down on me. I was getting to do both.

I made Missy Claire's bed with the most special care ever. I tucked. I smoothed. I yanked and folded. Each sheet corner was tight as wax to a barrel.

I took comfort in daydreaming that someday I'd be able to sleep in a feather bed of fine linens. I arranged each pillow just as Missy Claire likes it. She liked to say her bed pillows should be positioned as if they were "a throne of clouds for the head of an angel."

After the pillows, it was time for putting Missy Claire's china-headed dollies onto the bed. There were three of them dollies. They sat, side by side, on the settee in the corner. I propped the first two on Missy Claire's pillows.

The third dolly—I'd already named her Clove—was the prettiest of the three. She had molasses-colored hair and amber eyes. If she'd been a shade darker, she could have passed for nigra. When I lifted her from the settee, I couldn't help but hold her for a time. Even though her head was china, there was something soft about her, too. I folded her in my arms. I rocked her gently. I told her about Walnut. I told her about Serendipity.

Then I carefully set her on the bolster that topped Missy Claire's throne of clouds.

Soon as Mama gathered the remains of Gideon's breakfast tray, Missy Claire's brother arrived.

Thomas Farnsworth didn't do much talking, but, oh, was he ever lookin' things over. He was short and round-chested, with overgrown sideburns and possum eyes that watched every move we made. Missy Claire brought him right to the kitchen, where she sang praises over Mama's cooking. The whole time, Mama refused to even look in Thomas Farnsworth's direction. He was trespassing on her roost.

Missy Claire was blind to the whole thing. She was too busy telling Mama to serve tea cakes in the parlor, where she and Thomas would be spending the afternoon.

When Missy Claire and her brother left the kitchen, I saw Mama's jaw go tight. She got the same hard look as when I'd first shown her my lesson book—scared for what might be.

The afternoon crawled slow as an inchworm, with Mama keeping to herself through most of it. She made a supper of boiled pheasant for Missy Claire and her brother, and she served them with the careful hand that's expected for company. After supper she even rolled Thomas a twig of tobacco, and lit it so's he could smoke it.

Thomas Farnsworth didn't waste no time runnin' things. After we cleared the supper dishes, Missy Claire called Mama, Thea, and me together. She told us her brother had rented us out to Penelope Bates for making food and serving guests at the Christmas cotillion.

After Missy Claire was gone, Thea put a finger to her cheek. She shook her head. "I had me a special holy service planned, and now I gots to be watching a bunch of white folks get merry. The coming of the Savior's birth is meant for prayin', not party-makin'. Too much vice on Christmas Eve calls up haints and opens the door to evil. This cotillion ain't good. It ain't good, I tells you."

Mama didn't speak on the cotillion at all. Me, I was feeling two ways at once about it. Some of me was glad for the cotillion. A night in Doc Bates's warm parlor sure beat saying prayers with Thea in the drafty quarters, wishing with all my muster that Christmas would bring me a china-headed dolly.

But then there was a whole other piece of me that looked upon this cotillion—and Christmas—with sad eyes.

I never *would* have me a china-headed dolly, no matter how much wishing I did. And even though I'd been given the gift of learning letters, it was a gift I had to keep hidden. I couldn't show it off under the lighted tree candles as if it were a shiny new hair clip.

The Hobbs Hollow Christmas Cotillion was a party for young'uns and grown-ups alike. Girls my very own age would be dressed in velvet and lace, and soft-soled ball slippers. They would dance with each other, and would let their mamas rest so's their daddies could take *them* to the dance floor.

I would never dance with my daddy, and neither would my mama. (And surely Mama would have not a moment's rest this night.)

I could never even speak my pa's name, except when I was calling him "Master."

And when it came time for the holiday toast, I would try to swallow back my misery while everybody white drank in the sweetness of Mama's best-made eggnog.

24
ROSCO
December 22, 1862

HE'S HERE. SECESH TO THE BONE. Thomas Farnsworth.

Me and Clem were at the smithing shack picking clean Dash's hooves when we heard the bell. The holler bell, we called it, coming from the far fields. Only time that bell rang was when something couldn't wait— a haycock on fire, or somebody's child fallen into the well. Every slave on Parnell's place knew that when the holler bell sounded, you had to stop whatever you were doing and get to the smokehouse at the tobacco field's north end.

Lucky for Dash we were just about done picking. I turned Dash's back hoof free from between my knees. Clem threw his hoof pick to the dirt. "We'll take Dash to the stables on the way," he said. I gave Dash's hind quarters a slap. "Git, horse, the holler bell's calling."

The north end of the tobacco field stood on a slope of land, way past the toolshed. You could see the whole spread of the field from the stables. Dusk had started to sweep her cape across the sky. Up ahead in the distance, folks wove their way across Parnell's property. The brittle ground crackled under our feet. We stepped full and fast to meet the holler bell's clang.

Most everybody coming up on the smokehouse was breathing heavy, wondering 'bout the reason for the holler bell. Some of us were rubbing our hands to warm them from the cold.

At the smokehouse, Farnsworth was standing on a turned-over bucket, waiting for all of us to come inside. He stood among the hanging pork parts, which were stored in the smokehouse. Farnsworth looked like he belonged with those meats. He was just as pink as the rest of them.

As uppity as Missy Claire was, you'd have thought her brother would look like a king. But Thomas Farnsworth was as sloppy as they come. A scalawag in britches. His hair needed combing. His face needed a shave. His clothes could have used a good mend.

It wasn't until Clem and I got full into the smokehouse that I noticed it was only men in there, no women. No Mama. No Summer. No Thea. Once we had gathered—most all of Parnell's men—the holler bell grew silent. A rustle of voices filled the small stone house. Then Farnsworth spoke, and everybody got quiet.

"Listen good now," he said, "I'm going to tell you about the Farnsworth way."

Now I could see the resemblance between Missy Claire and her brother. It was in their way of talking. They both dragged their words when they spoke, like what they said was being pulled out slow from their way-back teeth.

"Look around you. There are no womenfolk here because I sent them all back to the quarters," he said. "What I got to say is for you only, because the Farnsworth way is the way of he-folk."

Even in the dim lantern light, I could see Clem's chest heaving. Me, I was waiting and watching and listening close.

"Gideon Parnell ran a profitable plantation. But my brother-in-law hasn't always been known for his ability to keep his slaves in line. I'm the one who first showed Gideon the proper way to lash a nigra, though I hear Gideon's slow to have his slaves meet the whip."

Farnsworth was talkin' real proud about himself, like he'd invented something. "I'm a longtime believer in the bullwhip, especially for breaking bucks like some of you," he said. "That's the Farnsworth way. Any buck who gives me even a speck of trouble can expect the leather from me." Farnsworth brought a whip out from behind his back. Biggest bullwhip I ever saw. Big as a boat rigging.

Clem flinched. He slowly backed away toward the

smokehouse door. Something was rising up in Clem. He was losing his good sense.

"I don't believe in whipping womenfolk," Farnsworth said. "I got my own way of dealing with them. Besides, it's bucks who give me the most trouble."

It was then that Farnsworth saw Clem backing up. He was looking right at Clem, and talking at him, too. "And there's always one buck—one at every plantation—who can't help but volunteer for a beating." Farnsworth stepped down from his bucket. He pushed past the rest of us to get to Clem. He snatched Clem by the collar. "I think I got me a volunteer right here," he said, his words dragging slow.

Now *my* chest was heaving. I heard myself praying silently to Thea's Almighty. I was scared for Clem. Scared Farnsworth would beat him to sawdust.

"Where you going, boy?" Farnsworth wanted to know. "Nobody—especially no darkie—backs out on me when I'm speaking."

Farnsworth let his whip uncoil. He still had Clem by the collar. "You see, men, this here is a buck who's begging to be whipped."

Farnsworth leaned in close to Clem. "Take your shirt off, boy."

Clem did what Farnsworth said. Did it without blinking. Peeled his shirt off his shoulders and let it drop.

A few of us raised our lanterns toward Clem. Even

in the dusk light, you could see Clem's back real good. You could see where Parnell's overseer had beat him before.

Clem's back was a spider web of whipping scars. Natty rinds of flesh. An ugly memory sewn deep into his skin.

Farnsworth slowly lowered the very tip of his whip and quietly traced Clem's scars with it. Same way a finger traces a map drawn into soft dirt. Farnsworth was teasing Clem with that whip. Frightening him with the torment of uncertainty.

Now I was praying to Thea's Almighty like I ain't never prayed before.

"There's no good flesh left on you, boy." Farnsworth was shaking his head. "Looks like somebody's whip has already taken care of you." He gave Clem a single shove. He swung open the smokehouse door and walked out into the night with his whip trailing behind him.

A small group of us rushed to Clem. I knelt to pick up Clem's shirt. When I handed it to him, he didn't take it. He just kept his eyes ahead, still hardly blinking.

The other men started to leave the smokehouse, till it was only me and Clem alone with the pork parts.

When everybody was gone, some kind of demon got a hold of Clem. He started talkin' crazy. Talkin' out of his head. His words flung into the empty darkness in an angry, mixed-up stream. Some of what he was saying made sense; some of it was gibberish. But there was no mistaking that Clem was speaking with a sure force—with a fever. He was trembling, spit flying when he spoke.

"Gots to *go*," he said. "I'll run till my feets fall off. North . . . North. Freedom wants me. Callin' my name, freedom is. Open wide, freedom, Clem's comin'— runnin', fightin', scratchin', bitin' to find you."

Clem was hugging himself. He was rocking with the heat of his own words. "Oh, freedom, you so sweet. I gots to get to you. *Gots* to! . . . . *Will* find you, free-dom—*will*. Any, any way I can. Won't stop till I do. Comin' to you, freedom—soon. Gettin' me *free*."

Clem crouched to the dirt floor. Under the single flickering light of my lantern, the dangling smokehouse meats made odd shadows against the stone walls. Clem pressed the heels of both hands to his forehead. He started to weep softly. "Gettin' me *free*."

I knelt beside Clem. This wasn't no demon dream. Thomas Farnsworth was a haint, come to life—come to *my* life.

Mama wasn't gonna wake me this time from night terrors and calling out in my sleep. All that I was seeing and feeling was real. A real I didn't want to live, even though I had me plenty of doubts about leaving Parnell's.

I helped Clem on with his shirt. He was still rocking and weeping. It was me who spoke next. "Gettin' *we* free."

25

Summer

December 24, 1862

G OODNESS LANDS!

I ain't never seen the likes of all the fancy footin' that graced the Bates parlor on Christmas Eve. All day it had been raining a cold, icy rain, but that didn't dampen the party one bit.

Miss Penelope, she was a sight. She was dressed in a watered silk gown the color of honey. Glistened like honey, too, that gown did. The whole room glistened.

Mama and I had dressed Missy Claire for the evening. Missy had chosen the emerald green with flounces. It was her first pick, and the best pick of all. Under the light of the parlor candles she was a true emerald. (The whole time spent at her vanity she'd complained to Mama about the rain. She'd urged Mama to make her curls tight enough to stay put.)

After Missy Claire was fully dressed, Mama and I

left to go to the Bates plantation, before the cotillion was to start. Miss Penelope told us we were to work 'longside the Bateses' house servants. She gave all of us a starched apron, and laid out each of our duties for the evening.

"Kit, I'm putting you in charge of the hors d'oeuvres. Arrange them as you would tea cakes, in spirals.

"Thea, you'll help serve the spirits. Make sure the glasses of my guests stay filled. At midnight, my husband will propose a holiday toast. As the hour approaches, see to it that each guest has a champagne flute filled and ready to raise.

"Summer, you'll be responsible for arranging all the confectionery items."

I didn't know what "confectionery items" were, but I nodded. "Yessum."

It wasn't until Miss Penelope left the room that I learned what I was supposed to do.

Mama said, "White folks always got to have fancy words for everything. All Miss Penelope had to say was for me to put the snacks real pretty on the tray, and for Summer to take care of the sweets."

Thea said, "I been servin' the spirits my whole life. And anybody who's walkin' with the *Holy* Spirit knows true spirits ain't found in no whisky glass."

I tugged at Mama. "*I'm* the one doin' the sweets?"

Mama set me clear, right quick. "You're puttin' the sweets out for the cotillion company, that's *all*. That don't mean tastin' or dreamin' on them sweets. Tonight's sweetnesses is for Miss Penelope's party, not for you."

"But, Mama, it's Christm—"

"You hard of hearin', child?"

I slid my hand into my apron pocket. "No, Mama."

I turned toward the larder to fetch a tray. But Mama stopped me short. "Summer, before you go gettin' all long in the face, let me give you something that's as sweet as any tea cake." Mama came up close behind me. She wrapped me in one of her hugs. She held me in that hug for a good, long squeeze.

With my arms folded inside of Mama's, I squeezed, too.

Mama kissed the top of my head. "Merry Christmas, Summer," she said softly.

Even though I wasn't allowed to taste none of the party sweets, I could sure dream on the sugared apple slices and honey-pears I was to serve throughout the evening. And I'd already put my eye to the crystal urn filled with hard candies that sat near the pianoforte in Miss Penelope's parlor. Them candies looked too pretty to eat. But, oh, they still set my mouth to watering.

The Bates home had a funny little clock that hung at the top of a long staircase. That clock had a regular face like the hall clock at Missy Claire's home. But Miss Penelope's clock was shaped like a house, and had a bird living inside—a chirping dolly bird that popped out on his nest!

First time I caught sight of that bird-clock was when it gave eight sudden chirps. That thing popped out all a'sudden, then jumped back, then popped out again, one time after another. Then that dolly bird stayed in its house while the clock chimes rang eight. Soon after, Miss Penelope's guests started comin' on.

The men came in frock coats and white gloves; the women in plumes and jewels and curls, and enough flounces to fill a hayloft. Each guest brought an ornament for the Bates Christmas tree. There was everything from whittled doves to bows of lace.

Thomas Farnsworth made a fine escort for Missy Claire. She was a whole head taller than her brother, but he had a way of mixing comfortably with people that must have rubbed off on Missy Claire, who I hadn't seen be as social since her days in the Arts and Letters Society.

Two guests were missing at the cotillion: Master Gideon and Doc Bates. And it was clear that 'most everybody at that party had an opinion about their absence. The opinions were quiet, but definite. I heard all kinds of whispers and hushed-up pity talk about Master Gideon. At least Parnell had him a good reason to be missing. But Doc Bates's absence was a mystery. Nobody, not even Miss Penelope, knew where the doctor was.

As I moved through the cotillion with my tray of sugared apple slices, I heard Miss Penelope telling folks that her husband had most likely made a "necessary exit" to tend to one of his patients. She said this was "typical of a doctor's duty," and that it was the duty of a doctor's wife was "to understand the inevitable," even on Christmas Eve.

But I don't know if Miss Penelope fully believed all what she was telling people. She was speaking the words and smiling, but her eyes said different.

As Mama hurried to fill another tray of fancy snacks, she told Thea, "That woman's hiding behind a doily of self-deceit."

Thea had just filled a new round of glasses. "She don't have the foggiest clue where her husband is."

By the time the bird-clock chirped ten, the cotillion was in full swing. One of Miss Penelope's house slaves— Ferd was his name—was playing the pianoforte. And another nigra—his name was Piper—played a fiddle. Not a sassy fiddle, the kind you jig to. He played a slow tune that floated on the night. White folks' music. It was pretty music, though. Made me feel warm and easy inside.

The music must have warmed the party guests, too, 'cause they danced. Danced real proper-like. Straight-back dancing. White folks' dancing. Even Missy Claire danced a time or two.

The Bateses' Christmas tree, covered with decorations, looked like it would grow right up to heaven if you peeled back the ceiling. Even that tree in all its finery seemed ready for a straight-back dance.

Mama and I were standing off by the staircase when Mama elbowed me. "Stop gawkin'," she said.

But I couldn't help it. I'd never seen grandness like what was at that cotillion, and I didn't want to miss none of it.

Miss Penelope kept on telling her company the doctor would be home soon, that he would never miss the midnight toast, even for the sake of some sickly soul.

Now, I don't know much about numbers or tellin' clock time by the clock's face, but I do know that two clock hands—one on top of the other—pointing straight to the sky means it's either high noon or midnight. Last I had counted the birdie's round of chirps, it had been eleven. Since then, I'd kept watching the clock hands. Kept watching the mama hand work its way to the baby hand, gettin' closer on midnight.

Still no Doc Bates.

Finally, when the mama clock hand was a hair's breadth from her baby, the doctor showed up. Seems he came out of nowhere. Just joined the party like he'd been there all along, eating sugared apple slices, enjoying fiddle music, and drinking spirits.

The birdie-clock gave twelve chirps. The cotillion guests gathered round Doc Bates, near the pianoforte. The doctor's face was flushed, and his hair looked windblown, but he didn't seem to be wet from the rain.

He took a flute glass from Thea's serving tray. A flute of golden bubbles. The fiddler rested his bow.

Miss Penelope hushed her company. She was grinning fully. Doc Bates raised his flute.

"Respected guests"—while Doc spoke, Miss Penelope had her hand to her heart and was taking a breath of relief—"here we stand to celebrate the birth of new life, the birth of our Savior. As we toast the coming of Christ, let us ponder the true meaning of salvation. To be truly saved is to conquer that which binds us— the hates, fears, and prejudices that stand as vexations to the soul.

"Tonight, let us ask ourselves, 'Do we love every man and woman as we love our own kin? What about the men—and the womenfolk—who are serving us tonight, and every other night? Do we see them as equal beings under the eyes of God?'

"There will surely come a day, my friends, when our maker will judge each and every one of us for the injustice of slavery. He may be judging us now. It is for this reason that I urge all of us to remember the Scripture that asks, 'For what shall it profit a man if he shall gain the whole world, and lose his own soul?'"

Doc Bates lifted his flute even higher. "Merry Christmas to all."

Now it was Mama who was gawking. Mama and Thea and me, too.

A strange silence hung among the guests. Not one of them made a move to salute the doctor's toast. Miss Penelope, her grin was gone. She was scowling and looking all bug-eyed at her husband. There was shame on her face.

I lowered my eyes, and when I did, I couldn't help but notice the doctor's shoes. They were soaked and muddy.

Finally, Miss Penelope cleared her throat. She lifted her flute of golden bubbles, bubbles that matched her dress. Her teeth were tight together. She said, "Yes, Merry Christmas to all."

Mama and Thea and I stayed till nearly daybreak cleaning up. When we returned our aprons to the hook inside Miss Penelope's scullery, I was truly sad.

Outside, the rain had cleared. Sun pierced a patch of clouds with raspberry bands of light. It was a bright Christmas morning, but for me, all the gleam of Christmas was over. I knew that as soon as we got back to the quarters, I would be left with the emptiness of expectations. I'd be left to wish on hard candy, lace bows, and fiddle music. Like every Christmas I had ever known, here came another one without shiny presents or a party to fill my day. At least I was good and tired, and I could look forward to the gift of sleep.

Back at the quarters, Mama went right to her prayer place. I fell to my pallet, curled myself to a baby's way of sleeping, and tucked my hands between both knees. Couldn't sleep, though. There was a lump under my pallet, right near my head. I thought it was the kerchief I'd balled up some days before. But when I turned back the pallet, there, gazing right up at me with black-button eyes, was a corncob dolly! She was tiny, no bigger than my hand. She had hair made from what looked like the strands of a horse's tail. That hair was sewn and braided, and beautiful. She even had little lips. Berry-juice lips, it looked like.

Sweetest little thing, that dolly. Sweeter than a whole mess of hard candy. I loved her right away. I hugged her to me. Hugged her so close, I could have near to broken her little cob body.

Didn't even have to think on a name. Her name was Cornelia. Cornelia, my Christmas dolly. I never stopped to wonder where Cornelia came from. I just held her and held her.

All my weariness, my bone-tired, went away with the joy of Cornelia. It was a good thing, too, 'cause Thea was summoning us for Christmas Day prayers.

I was still wearing the house dress I'd worn to the cotillion. I tucked Cornelia into my pocket and headed toward the meeting quarters, where Thea was waiting.

When I got there, Mama had her face to Thea's shoulder. Soon as Thea saw me come in, that's when she told everybody gathered that Rosco and Clem were gone.

26
ROSCO
December 24, 1862

CLEM AND ME, WE HELD HANDS. We were racing time. We had to get as far as we could from Parnell's before dawn showed her face. Before morning betrayed us with her light.

Clem and I had fled as soon as Mama and Summer had left for the Bates cotillion. Between the two of us we had a single haversack with a half-dried ash-cake and a hunk of salt pork wrapped inside.

This was the blackest night ever. No moon. No stars. No Diamond Eye to guide us. And that rain! It was a prickly winter rain, slamming down hard as nails.

We took the backwoods behind the smokehouse. Steep woods, thick with underbrush, heavy with mud. Didn't matter none how steep them woods were or how prickly the rain. Clem and me were gettin' us free. We ran till there wasn't no more hill left, till the land lay flat again. We made it to a clearing, a spread of field that opened onto the headwaters of the Rappahannock River.

The wind in my chest was going sharp. I let go of Clem. With the back of my hand, I wiped the wet from my face. "Clem, I need to stop a moment. I gotta get my breath."

"Ain't no time to stop, Rosco. We're at Holly Glen, where they caught Marietta and me. It's too wide open here to stop runnin' now. Just up yonder we're comin' to a narrow place in the river, where help's waitin'. Keep with me, now, Rosco. Keep with me."

For some reason, I was thinking on Summer then, wishing I could see the surprise spreading across her face when she caught sight of the corncob dolly I'd made for her. I let thoughts of Summer's happiness fill me. Something 'bout seeing Summer's smile in my mind made my breath come easier. "I'm with you, Clem."

Clem led me to an abandoned shanty, pulled me inside, and we crouched together in a potato hole. I'd never seen dark like this. Dead dark. I tried to blink it back, but all my eyes allowed me was black on black on black. Clem was whispering, "*Now* we stop—stop and wait."

I felt safe next to Clem. Safe in the warmth of being close to him. I closed my eyes and settled to the black stillness all around. Summer came to me again, this time as a memory. The memory of learning letters. The sweet recollection of one nigra girl's wish to read. Even with Summer's up-jumpy way, she was startin' to see words.

I thought on a lot of things in that hole. I thought on Lowell's courage, and on Master Gideon Parnell, who had been lucky enough to witness his son's bravery, even if he couldn't recognize it.

Soon my thoughts tumbled to Mama. To tea cakes. To a woman whose hands knew all kinds of healing.

Strong as strong gets. *Mama.*

I remembered then what Mama told me—the best way to feel safe in darkness is to speak words that comfort you.

The one word that was there for me right then in that potato hole was the word that had always brought me peace: *Mama.*

So, I prayed silently in the name of my mother, hoping Mama's strong-as-strong-gets would fill me up and keep me going, like it always did.

Mama . . . Mama . . . Mama . . .

Clem was trembling beside me. Trembling and sniffing back the cold night. Now I took his hand and gave it a squeeze. I wanted to tell Clem to find his own special word to say, but I thought it best we not speak.

Seems we were in that hole till the end of forever. What we were waiting for, I didn't fully know. But Clem knew. I *knew* he knew. And I trusted him.

My legs were folded firm beneath me. Just as they were giving in to the numbness of sleep, a lantern shone into the shanty. Its tiny light swept once over us, then back again. Clem tensed. I kept with my unspoken prayer.

Mama . . . Mama . . . Mama . . .

The light glowed again. Quick, then gone. But this time a whistle came behind it. A soft whistle from somebody's lips. Two short, thin spots of sound, then quiet.

Clem and me, we were still as stone. The pattern rose again—*lantern, whistle, quiet*—and once more after that. *Lantern—whistle—quiet.* On the third time around, Clem whistled back, low and fast.

The light moved closer, and stayed. It brought on the shadow of a man. A voice sprang up in the dark. "Who goes there?"

Clem's body loosened at the voice's call. He slid his hand from mine. Now the lantern's flame hovered above us, casting the man into greater darkness as he lowered his lantern toward the potato hole. "Who goes, I say?"

Clem spoke up then. "Doc Bates, you came!"

The lantern backed away, just enough to light the man's chin and nose. It *was* Doc Bates. It was his lips, set in that smile of contentment. He reached to give each of us a hand out of the hole. When he saw me, he gently clapped my shoulder. "My wagon is outside.

We *must* hurry. A medical man can only take the guise of his duties so far. My wife is consumed with her cotillion. She's grown accustomed to my unpredictable night departures in the name of tending the sick, but tonight my alibi grows increasingly thin as midnight approaches, when I'm to deliver the Christmas Eve toast."

Doc Bates was wearing a mackintosh coat and a tarp draped around his head and face to keep him dry. "As I approached the shanty, I believe the town clock was striking eleven. I'd hoped to arrive sooner, but I was slowed by this blasted rain," he said. "If I can just get you boys across the river, you'll be fine for a time. A little more than ten miles north of here, there's a lady who makes brooms, Talley Pembroke is her name. She occupies a small cabin—a cabin with a broom hung on the front door—just south of Arlington. She's a steadfast believer in the movement. She's helped many fugitives, even the woman they call Moses, Harriet Tubman herself."

We loaded onto the back of Doc Bates's wagon, where he hid us under a bushel of onions and a feed sack of grain. The doctor threw a blanket over us. He tucked the blanket tight at the inside edges of the wagon bed. "Rest now," he said. "You've got risky days ahead of you."

Even with the bumps and thrusts of the wagon wheels under my head, I let myself sink into hopefulness.

Soon into the ride, the wagon wheels came to a sudden stop. I could hear Doc Bates clucking his tongue at his horse, Judd. But we stayed stopped. The wagon jerked, then shimmied. Doc Bates's horse sounded a grunt from deep in his belly. Doc Bates swore. He came to the wagon bed, where he spoke to us through the blanket. "We're at the place where the river begins to shallow, but the river's swollen. Judd has gone skittish on me. When water rises to a point, it frightens Judd, makes him downright obstinate. It'll take the bulk of General Robert E. Lee's Eastern Confederate army to move Judd now."

Clem called out from under the onions, "Is he rearing, digging his hooves?"

The horse grunted a second time. "That's it exactly," Doc Bates said.

"Coddle him," I called back.

Doc Bates tried to coax Judd, but the doctor was going about it all wrong. I could tell by the herky motion of the wagon, and the horse's snorting, that Doc Bates was yanking Judd's rein. Clem must have felt it, too. We both wriggled free of the blanket and stepped down off the wagon bed, back into the rain. Clem told Doc Bates to stand at Judd's mount side while he and I stood on each side of Judd's head.

The land beneath our feet was what Thea used to call sow's heaven—mud thick as molasses. Judd's whole muzzle had gone tight. He gnashed his teeth. He was railing against all of us trying to wheedle him. Judd was just plain spooked. I tried to calm him. "Easy now. *Easy*, boy." Judd looked to be seventeen hands, at least. His size alone made it hard to budge him.

"We ain't got time for sweet-talk," Clem said. "We gotta move him forward, best way we can." Clem gave a single tug at Judd's bridle.

"He's too stymied, Clem," I said. "The best way to encourage him is to still him first. Sweet-talk will get us across this river faster than anything else." I patted Judd.

Then Doc Bates threw in his dib. "I know Judd better than anyone knows him. It's no use. We should turn back, return to the shanty. You boys can spend the night there, hide out during the day tomorrow—it'll be Christmas; folks won't be about—then you can try again when night falls. Hopefully, the rain will let up, and the river will recede." Doc Bates shuddered against the cold. He pulled his makeshift hood close around his face. He said, "As far as I can see, going back is the only way."

Clem snatched at Judd's bridle again. "I *ain't* turnin' back—not now. Not ever. We'll wade across."

The rain was flying down in spikes. It was freezing rain. The meanest kind of rain there is. That thorny rain hurling from the sky made things worse for poor Judd. He kept swishing his tail, trying to swat off the icy bother.

Doc Bates urged Clem. "The waters are too rough, and much too cold. If you try to wade across, you'll be washed to the rocks, or die of hypothermia. And even if we make it across in the wagon, I've scant the time to get home. We can't do it tonight. I'm imploring you to listen to reason."

But Clem was past the point of listening. He kept tugging and tugging, and riling Judd.

That's when I started in with singing softly.

"I'll meet you in the mornin'
When I reach the promised land . . ."

I don't know how "Old Chariot" knew to come to me then, but it came with a force as strong as the rain. Surest way to ease a stubborn horse.

"On the other side of Jordan,
For I's bound for the promised land."

Clem came to my side of the horse. He got right up in my face. "What in *damnation* are you doing?"

"I'm settling Judd so's we can cross."

"This ain't no parlor game, Rosco. Keep with your foolin', and you're gonna get us killed out here." Clem huffed. "Slave catchers love to brag. And the catchers round here will have a good time tellin' folks 'bout the fool nigras they found at the river."

"I *ain't* foolin', Clem. Singing's what softens a mule-headed horse."

Clem's mouth was all twisted. "I was right about you, Rosco. You ain't nothin' but a critter. I should have left you behind." Clem shoved me. Shoved me hard.

I shoved Clem back. "You want to fight me, Clem? Right here in the rain? On Christmas Eve? With a swelled-up river, a white man who don't feel like waiting around, and a stubborn horse, solid as a smokehouse, got his hooves dug into the mud?" Now I was up in Clem's face. I shoved him a second time. "C'mon, then, Clem, fight me."

Clem startled backward. But it was what Doc Bates did next that surprised Clem even more. Doc Bates took my lead. He started in singing. Quietly, but enough so's Judd could hear.

"When that old chariot comes,
I'm going to leave you,
I'm bound for the promised land,
Friends, I'm going to leave you."

Judd got real still. He nosed the water. Then he stepped in, enough to cover his front hooves. Clem went back to Judd's other side. He curled his fingers around the rein and guided Judd's steps. I joined Doc Bates in singing.

"I'm sorry, friends to leave you,
Farewell! Oh, farewell!"

Judd was trying to find his footing. He stepped careful, but steady. Clem wasn't singing, but his lips couldn't help but shape the words. Judd moved past us, further into the water. Doc Bates mounted to his driver's seat. He motioned us back to the wagon, where we buried ourselves under the onions and grain.

With his backbone pressed to mine, Clem surrendered to his own mule-headedness. He sang softly with Doc Bates and me.

"But I'll meet you in the morning,
Farewell! Oh, farewell!"

27
Summer
December 31, 1862

A NEW YEAR'S COMIN', but something in me feels older.

Soon after Rosco and Clem got to be missing, Thomas Farnsworth sent out a pack of search dogs to find them. He gave Rance, Parnell's overseer, a snatch of Clem's shirttail and a tattered patch from Rosco's britches. "Have your dogs sniff out every twig and burrow from here to the Potomac," he ordered. "Do whatever it takes to find those two."

On the day after Christmas, the catchers came back, saying they got as far as the Rappahannock, but because of the cold and the rain, the dogs lost Clem's and Rosco's scent. Rance told Farnsworth there was no use in keeping up the hunt. "Them boys is long past gone," he said.

Mama worked sadly and silently in the cookhouse. When she wasn't workin', she went off to her prayer place, usually in the late-night hours and early morning, right before Chief got to crowing.

Today Mama and Thea took to polishing everything in the front hall—the doorknobs, the spindle-back bench, the standing clock—which were usually Rosco's house duties. Mama put me to polishing the balusters, another one of Rosco's chores. The three of us worked quietly, sullenly. Mama was the one who spoke first. Spoke like she'd been mulling on her thoughts. "I know Thomas Farnsworth's kind," she said. "Same kind as Briggs Thornton, the master who sold me to Gideon. Them's white folks with hard, hard hearts. If they bring back them boys, they'll bring 'em back dead. Ain't no question about it."

There was hurt in Mama's eyes like I ain't never seen in my mother. I looped my dust rag over the banister so's I could take a rest on the bottom step. But I wanted Mama to rest, too. I took her hand and held it. "Come sit with me, Mama."

Mama shook her head. "Ain't no room for slackin'," she said. "We's got to keep with our work."

I tugged on Mama's hand. "Only for a minute, Mama."

When I coaxed Mama to the stair step, I said to Thea, "Mama and me, we need us a solid prayer."

Thea came to the steps and bowed her head. I lowered my head too. Mama followed. I was still holding Mama's hand.

Thea set to praying. "Almighty Lord, watch over young Rosco and Clem. Guide their feet to safe soil. Show them. Protect them. Work in and through their eager spirits. And help us, Lord, to have faith in the promise of freedom for all of us still living here at Parnell's plantation. In your Almighty name, we pray. Amen."

When Thea's prayer was through, Mama and I spoke at the same time. "Amen," we said softly.

When we got back to work, Thea told Mama and me that her prayer was already working. "Rosco and Clem have reached higher ground. I know it in my marrow," she said.

A piece of calm came to Mama's eyes, and Thea went on and on about Rosco and Clem, and how she was for certain they were "safe in the everlasting arms."

Later, in the quarters, I wondered about Thea's strange ways. How could she know things she couldn't fully see?

Then an odd little thing happened. Something that gave me reason to take up a kernel of belief in Thea's know-how.

In the days after Rosco and Clem fled, Cornelia, my corncob dolly, was the only one who brought me true comfort. Every morning, after Mama left the quarters, I propped Cornelia on the oak stool near my pallet, so's I could do all kinds of talking to her. I told her how my belly had a hurt deep as Parnell's well, from missing

Rosco and Clem. Told her I didn't know if I could keep up with learning letters without Rosco. Told her I didn't rightly know if I even wanted to bother. Cornelia, she listened good, took in all my grief.

But when I got to talking about giving up on letters, Cornelia fell clean off the stool. She landed facedown with a tiny smack, right onto my pallet. On the spot where I lay my head, near where she had been hiding on Christmas morning when I first found her.

In falling, Cornelia's little dress flipped up its skirt, turning it back like a hand playing peekaboo. That's when I saw them—tiny letters embroidered onto the underside of Cornelia's skirt. Tiny letters that danced along her hem.

Them letters were dancing for me. They were tellin' me something. They were making words I knew, words I'd seen before.

My dolly's dress hem said, *Summer is a blooming flower.*

The embroidery stitches were jagged, but they'd been put in place with the care of a hand that was trying its best. And them stitches, them special words, were all for me.

It was Cornelia's dress hem that eased me to trusting on Thea's wisdom. Maybe she was right about Rosco and Clem. Maybe the two of them had made it to some better place. Maybe they were in Serendipity, the promised land, where there ain't no masters or hatred. Where everything's beautiful.

Them embroidered words made it hard to think on nothing but good. Especially with all the mutterings about. Ever since Rosco had told us that Abraham Lincoln was planning to put his name to a freedom paper, I'd heard more and more folks saying it was really gonna happen. Gonna happen on New Year's Day, people said. Folks were calling Lincoln's paper the Emancipation Proclamation, a paper that said all nigras livin' under the Confederacy would be free. Every single one of us—free. Just like that.

Some of the Parnell slaves—mostly older folks—said we shouldn't put no trust in such pig-slop, that the whole thing was all a big hoax.

But Thea, she had her seer-woman view on things. "Freedom's comin' ahead at the horizon," she said. "I can feel it from deep down."

The hearsay about the president's proclamation had everybody in a stew. When Thomas Farnsworth heard that the proclamation was soon to be official—he got wind of it soon after Rance told us Clem and Rosco weren't nowhere to be found—he had Mama pack his satchel so's he could go back home to Louisiana. Right before Missy Claire's brother left, he swore the South was dying a slow death. "We're surely losing the war, and now this threat of freeing the slaves," he'd said. Then he said he had no choice but to leave Parnell's so's he could keep his own plantation in order till "the final sickening demise."

Missy Claire begged Thomas to stay on, but he refused. He left just as he came, possum eyes lookin' every which way. Once her brother was gone, Missy returned to her days in the parlor. Mama was pleased as pie to see Thomas Farnsworth go. She went right back to running things, the way she'd done after Parnell got his heart-shock.

This morning, when Mama brought Missy her tea service—I followed behind Mama, carrying the place linens—Missy spoke real firm to Mama. She said, "Kit, don't you believe a single word of that ridiculous gossip about the president's intentions. All this talk that's been circulating is nothing but political conjecture. You're to pay the rumors no attention. Is that clear?"

Mama set Missy Claire's tray in front of her. She didn't answer Missy one way or the other. She just poured her tea. Then, as Mama turned to leave, Missy Claire spoke again, more gently this time. She said, "You know, Kit, you can be free right here with us. There's no good reason to ever leave this plantation— ever. Besides, you're pretty much a free woman right now, anyway."

I saw Mama flinch. She stood in the parlor doorway for a long moment. She kept her back to Missy Claire. Finally, she spoke. "No, Missy Claire, I'm *not* truly free. But my mind is free, and I'm free to *make up* my mind anyways I want. So, if Mr. Lincoln's 'mancipation comes to pass, I'll use my God-given free will to decide where freedom suits me best."

Missy Claire was stunned to silence. She folded her arms tight in front of her. She made her way to the parlor window, parted the curtains, and stared out.

That night, when all was quiet in the quarters, I whispered soft to Cornelia, "Mama is a blooming flower, just like me."

28
ROSCO
December 25, 1862

THE STINK OF ONIONS HAD settled to my clothes, but at least the rain had stopped. Morning was cold and clear and new. Me and Clem had traveled on foot till we found the cabin with the broom on the door. When we knocked, a little white woman answered. Wasn't no more taller than I was, that woman. She had tiny teeth the color of butter, and a smile as big as the Rappahannock. Her face was bright, with straight-at-you eyes, blue like the morning sky. She seemed glad to see us. "Thank goodness!" she exclaimed. "Firewood, firewood! I prayed for firewood, and here it is on my doorstep. A Christmas wish come true."

The little white woman hurried us inside. She was talkin' fast, like she had a lot to say at once. We couldn't get a word in, couldn't ask if we'd come to the right place. "You boys look hungry. Sit a spell—eat. And then we'll get on with the firewood." A small table with three chairs stood toward the back of the cabin, near the hearth. The woman slid two of the chairs away from the table. She slapped their seats, then settled herself to the third chair. "Sit now," she said, "rest a spell."

All kinds of brooms hung from the walls and ceiling. Clem's eyes were shifting from me to the brooms to the butter-toothed lady. Finally he asked, "Are you Talley Pembroke?" She reared back on the haunches of her chair, so far back that I thought she'd tip over and land on her head. But she had full control of her chair, even as it wavered. "I'm as Talley Pembroke as they come. Who are you?" she wanted to know. She came back to sitting on all four legs of her chair. She leaned in on one elbow and studied both of us.

"My name's—" I started to answer, but Clem raised a hand to stop me.

"Never mind who we are. Dr. Horace Bates sent us to see you."

Now Talley Pembroke raised a hand—raised two hands—to shush Clem. "No need explaining." She rose from her seat, rummaged through the larder, and returned with a slab of corn bread and half a boiled chicken. Me and Clem wolfed that food like tomorrow wasn't ever gonna come. Sure beat a rain-soaked ash-cake and a hunk of salt pork that had gone cold.

When the last of the chicken was gone, Talley handed Clem an ax. "There's a pile of wood out back that needs busting. You chop"—she pointed two fingers at me—"and your friend here, he'll stack."

Clem stood up sharply. "You got it all wrong. We're here for—"

Talley folded her hands in front of her on the table. "I know *just* why you're here. And as much as I'd like to sit and shoot the winter breeze with you two, I can't afford to. I'm suspect all over this county. Any colored who comes to me has got to give the appearance they work for me." Talley pulled two coats off a pair of hooks in the corner and offered the coats to us. "The best show of work is *hard* work. Work nobody can question."

So we worked. We chopped and stacked all day, taking turns with the ax. Come dusk, I thought I would drop from exhaustion. And come nightfall, I nearly did. Talley let us quit only when the sky grew too dark to see. I stoked her fire while she fixed us a supper of mashed turnips and more corn bread.

While we ate at her table, she gave us our instructions for moving on. It was all I could do to keep from sleeping right then and there. "Traveling at night is best," Talley said. "Tonight you'll sleep by my fire for a time, then I'll wake you so you still have a solid stretch of darkness left."

Clem was fixed to every word Talley spoke. His eyes never left hers. "Follow the river till you come to a marshy stretch of land. You'll then be near Mount Harmony, Maryland, coming onto the Chesapeake Bay.

You can't miss the mighty Chesapeake. It's big water. When the trees start to get mossy at the roots, you'll know you're close. At daybreak—just before the sun peeks up at the horizon—a Quaker man, Wendell Hearn, will be waiting for you along the banks. He sails fugitives on his fishing boat up the bay to Baltimore."

I was full to listening now. I took a bite of corn bread. I chewed slowly. I paid close attention. "How will we know this Wendell Hearn?" I asked.

"Hearn makes like an owl—three single hoots—that's his secret signal. Listen for the call, and follow it until you find him. When you get to Baltimore, there will be another boat waiting, a dinghy operated by a man who will row you toward barn lanterns with colored shades—a yellow light and blue light on shore."

The fire in Talley's cabin was beginning to falter. The flame sputtered and hissed. Not Clem or me made a move to stoke it. We didn't want to miss one single detail from Talley.

"When you're back on land, you'll have to travel by foot. You'll be just south of Pennsylvania then. Stay low and quiet in those parts. And keep off the roads. The region is what some folks have come to call the 'freedom line,' the place where Maryland crosses into Pennsylvania, into freemen's country. Once you're over the line, you can travel a bit more safely, as far north as you please, to New York, Connecticut, Massachusetts."

Talley got up to fix the fire. She kept talking as she

poked at the embers. She hoisted one of our just-cut logs into the smolder. She stood by the fireplace until the flame returned. "There's all kinds of bloodthirst in and around the freedom line," she warned. "Bounty hunters, hungry for runaways. And hound dogs who are just plain hungry. At every turn, always remember vigilance, prudence, careful timing."

Talley brought our haversack up from under her table. "I've packed you enough food to last you plenty. Promise me that when you reach freedom, you'll help others reach it, too. And that you'll tell them how to find Talley Pembroke."

Clem and I nodded agreement.

We did just what Talley said. Did it to the letter. Did it with vigilance, prudence, careful timing, and a heap of luck. For nearly two days, we kept a steady pace, and didn't snag on no trouble. Wendell Hearn told us that the route we were following was one of the most foolproof of any along the Underground Railroad. Clem later swore it was the Diamond Eye that guided us safely. I thought it was all that praying I'd done in the potato hole.

We walked up on Pennsylvania at first light. It truly was a promised land, set out before us on a morning I would remember for a long time coming. Twilight spread through the trees in the same way a horn announces the arrival of greatness. The sun arched her

long fingers over a grassy crest. If I hadn't known better, I would have bet my britches that somebody had
put a shine to the day with some kind of silver polish.
Everywhere I looked—the trees, the leaves, the land,
the sky—things seemed to glitter.

When we came to a wide-open meadow, Clem
stepped ahead of me to be welcomed by its beauty. All
it took was two words from Clem, and my heart was a
pounding drum inside my chest.

"We's free."

EPILOGUE
ROSCO
January 1, 1863

I AIN'T NEVER SEEN so many colored folk gathered in one place. Too many nigras to count. And these were high-hat coloreds. Free men and women, dressed fine and proper. Colored who had enjoyed freedom's advantages. It was as if the Almighty had assembled us for the occasion, and had set me and Clem down in the middle of the hullabaloo to revel in the gladness.

We'd been waiting inside the packed hall of Tremont Temple since sundown, when, at about ten o'clock, a messenger hurried into the hall. "It's coming! It's on the wires!" he shouted. Soon after, a telegram came—the proclamation!

Frederick Douglass himself came to hear the news. Douglass was a man of unforgettable stature. A big man. Bold and proud. It was clear he didn't shy back for nobody. His hair was a swell of cotton that haloed his face. He was dressed proper as a white man—waistcoat, cravat, starched shirt, and shoes shiny as a lookin' glass. Clem nudged me. "That there's a colored king," he said.

And, oh, could Douglass ever speak. It was clear he had been schooled in the ways of oration. When he addressed the crowd—when he told us that President Abraham Lincoln's signed-and-official Emancipation Proclamation would be delivered at any moment—he brought slow, deliberate music to each and every word. When the proclamation finally arrived, Douglass had to hush the excited crowd who kept interrupting the reading of the document with joyous shouts.

Finally, the audience settled. We grew as quiet as the winter air, letting true delight settle upon us. When the part of Lincoln's pronouncement that said ". . . I do order and declare that all persons held as slaves . . . are, and henceforward shall be, free . . ." was read, the crowd broke into another wild cheer. Whoops and hollers rang through all of Boston. Menfolk threw their hats high in the air. Women did the same—they let loose their bonnets. People were hugging and happy and giddy and dancing. Even grown men cried at the wonder of it all.

But there was more to Lincoln's proclamation. A provision that, judging by the thankful grin crossing Frederick Douglass's face, pleased him greatly. The document said that henceforth freed slaves ". . . of suitable condition . . ." would be ". . . received into the armed service of the United States to garrison forts, positions, stations, and other places, and to man vessels of all sorts in said service."

Even though the Union had allowed colored men to enlist in their army before this day, hearing these words from our president made it all more official, somehow. Frederick Douglass, our colored king, led us in singing "Blow Ye the Trumpet, Blow!" and he told the crowd that any man among us would have his full and complete assistance in enlisting for military duty.

Clem locked me in the crook of his elbow. He hugged me to him. "Glory be!" I shouted. "Praise freedom's name! Coloreds to arms!"

Clem raised both his fists. "To arms, to arms!" he called.

All of us nigras gathered on this day—men, women, young'uns, and old folk—had finally come to freedom. Some had been born to freedom. Others had bought their way free. Many had escaped, like Clem and me, who'd come to freedom by way of "Old Chariot," the kindness of white folks, the Diamond Eye, and the Almighty's good grace.

A Note from the Author

I AM AN AFRICAN AMERICAN. That means the branches of my family tree spread back to a time when slavery was an institution in the United States. It means I have grown up with a distinguished legacy of men and women who have spent their lives fighting for freedom, and whose names, though not officially logged on the pages of history, are integral to the shaping of America.

One of the many blessings of this rich cultural heritage is that I grew up hearing the same message over and over again: *Search. Study. Find. Know the history of your people.* As a result, I have become an avid history buff, reading all I can about American history as it relates to black people.

Silent Thunder: A Civil War Story began just this way. Sometime around the spring of 1996, I happened on a photograph of a black boy named Jackson, a slave, who became a drummer with the United States Colored Troops. I was immediately struck by the intensity of young Jackson's gaze. That child—he appeared to be no more than thirteen—looked proud to be part of the Civil War effort. (The photograph came from the Massachusetts Commandery Military Order of the Loyal Legion and the U.S. Army Military History Institute.)

Years prior, I had discovered a similar vintage photograph of an unidentified girl, seated near a woodpile, embracing a handmade doll. Her expression—she looked directly at the viewer—held the same intrigue as the photograph of Jackson. This girl had a spark of eager inquisitiveness in her eyes. And, it was clear that she loved her dolly.

Both images stayed with me. Who were these children? I wondered. What kinds of lives did they lead? How did they express their deepest desires? Whatever became of them?

There was only one way to answer these questions for myself: turn these bright-eyed children into characters I could shape and come to know better.

Jackson became Rosco Parnell. The anonymous girl became his sister, Summer. There was no question that I would set *Silent Thunder* during the Civil War and during the time period when the Underground Railroad was running at its peak. What better backdrop to build a story, with these two characters at its very center?

In 1861, when the first shots of the Civil War were fired, one of the most fascinating periods in America's history began. The war that came to be called "the War between the States" was fought between eleven Southern states that had seceded from the United States of America—the Confederacy—and the Northern Union States, those states that stayed in the Union. Like any war, the Civil War was a war about differences. The South fought to preserve its agricultural economy, which depended on maintaining slavery. The North sought to industrialize, which depended on wage labor. And, many Northerners felt that slavery was inherently wrong, and wanted to end it.

To the nearly four and a half million black people living in the North and South, the Civil War was a war about slavery, a war they wanted to fight. But white folks had other ideas. Many thought slavery was not the issue at all. They called it "a white man's war" and believed that African Americans had no business in it.

But the black men and women of the time refused to sit back and let this war, whose outcome they felt directly affected their lives, be fought without them. When the Union began to accept black people into its army, young, brave men were eager to take up arms. By the time the Civil War ended in 1865, nearly 180,000 African Americans had served.

Silent Thunder: A Civil War Story is fiction built on a foundation of facts. The Parnell family, the Parnell slaves, and their neighbors are my own creation, but many of the incidents surrounding their lives are based on real events.

The town of Hobbs Hollow is also fictional, but it is based on actual small towns in the state of Virginia. As was true in the 1860s, I have attempted to show

how, even under the shroud of slavery, the lives of black people and white people were often stitched together like the threads and patches of an intricate quilt.

The Civil War battles in *Silent Thunder*, and the dates on which these battles occurred, are real. Also true is the occurrence of grave snatchers stealing the bodies of dead soldiers for study at a medical school in Winchester, Virginia.

During the Civil War, people looked to newspapers for updates on the war's progress. *Harper's Weekly* was one of the most widely read news journals of the time. Similarly, several newspapers were created by free blacks, with the purpose of providing those African Americans who could read with a black perspective on the events of the day. The New Orleans newspaper *L'Union*, and the "Men of my blood!" article, published on December 6, 1862, did exist.

A portion of Rosco and Clem's escape route—sailing up the Chesapeake Bay to Baltimore with the help of a Quaker man; riding in a dinghy toward colored barn lights on the shore—is based on documented accounts from Harriet Tubman's many trips along the Underground Railroad.

President Abraham Lincoln did create a draft of his Emancipation Proclamation, which was originally presented to Congress on September 22, 1862. From that time, right up until the final document was issued on January 1, 1863, there was tremendous speculation and debate about it.

The formal Emancipation Proclamation was indeed read at Tremont Temple, in Boston. Frederick Douglass, the noted black abolitionist leader, a former slave who devoted his life to the fight for equal rights, attended the reading of the Emancipation Proclamation before a crowd of nearly three thousand black people who were holding a vigil, waiting for news that the president had signed his name to the document.

Though many of us who write historical fiction take great care in researching the day-to-day details and the political events of bygone eras, we can never fully know the true impact these events had on the souls of those who lived them.

We can never know the degrading injustice of having to hide one's desire to read—of being shackled with the burden of illiteracy.

We can never know the sting of tears shed for family members sold off at auction.

We can never know the intense yearning for freedom that burned in the hearts of so many enslaved people.

It is only through books that we can glimpse the joys and sufferings experienced by those who came before us. And it is through these same books that we can look to the past to gain insight into the future, so that the history buffs of tomorrow can shape the events of history today.

Andrea Davis Pinkney
July 1998
New York City

Bibliography

I CONSULTED MANY BOOKS on the Civil War period for the creation of this novel. The following are those I found most helpful, those I referred to several times over. I cite them here with tremendous gratitude for the men and women who wrote them:

Foner, Philip S. *The Life and Writings of Frederick Douglass, Volume III, The Civil War 1861–1865.* International Publishers Co. Inc., New York: 1952.

Gorsline, Douglas. *What People Wore: A Visual History of Dress from Ancient Times to the Early Twentieth Century.* Dover Publications, Mineola, New York: 1980.

Haskins, Jim. *Black, Blue & Gray: African Americans in the Civil War.* Simon & Schuster, New York: 1998.

Haskins, Jim. *Get on Board: The Story of the Underground ...d.* Scholastic, New York: 1993.

Igus, Toyomi, ed. *Book of Black Heroes, Volume Two: Great Women in the Struggle.* Just Us Books, Orange, New Jersey: 1991.

Lester, Julius. *To Be a Slave.* Dial Books, New York: 1968.

McFeely, William S. *Frederick Douglass.* W.W. Norton & Company, Inc., New York: 1991.

Mellon, James, ed. *Bullwhip Days: The Slaves Remember, an Oral History.* Weidenfeld & Nicholson, New York: 1988.

Meltzer, Milton, ed. *Frederick Douglass: In His Own Words.* Harcourt Brace & Company, 1995: San Diego, California: 1995.

Meltzer, Milton, ed. *Lincoln: In His Own Words.* Harcourt Brace & Company, 1995: San Diego, California: 1993.

National Park Service. *The Underground Railroad.* U.S. Department of the Interior, Washington, D.C.: 1998.

Taylor, M. W. *Harriet Tubman.* Chelsea House Publishers, New York: 1991.

Trudeau, Noah Andre. *Like Men of War: Black Troops in the Civil War 1862–1865.* Little, Brown & Company, Boston: 1998.